DOGO-GRAPHY

THE LIFE AND ADVENTURES

OF THE

CELEBRATED DOG TIGER,

COMPRISING

A VARIETY OF AMUSING AND INSTRUCTIVE EXAMPLES, ILLUSTRATIVE
OF THE HAPPY EFFECTS OF THE APPROPRIATE TRAINING
AND EDUCATION OF DOGS,

BY FRANCIS BUTLER,
Author of the "Spanish Teacher" and "French Speaker:" Teacher and
Translator of Languages; 205 Water-street, New-York.

"Go, get thee hence, and find my dog again."
SHAKSPEARE.

"'Tis sweet to hear the watch-dog's honest bark
Bay deep-mouthed welcome, as we draw near home."
BYRON.

STEREOTYPE EDITION.

NEW-YORK:
PUBLISHED BY FRANCIS BUTLER, 205 WATER-STREET,
AND SOLD BY ALL BOOKSELLERS.

1856.

PRINTED BY D. FANSHAW,
85 Ann-st. cor. Nassau.

CONTENTS.

CONTENTS.

CONTENTS.

PREFACE.

Old TIGER's *biographical* object (it appears) in introducing us to so many of his *most respectable* canine acquaintances, is to demonstrate, by his own personal experience, the absolute necessity of a radical reform in the management, training, and education of dogs; displaying the mutual advantages thereby insured to both teacher and scholar; also, to induce his superiors to rescue his dishonored race from unmerited neglect and degradation.

Should his humble endeavors prove successful, he will raise a lasting monument to the memory of the most deserving quadruped that ever worried a cat or saved the life of his master.

INTRODUCTION.

Who will introduce me to the man who has not been struck with the wonderful instinct, sagacity and fidelity of the Dog? Yet, what domestic animal is the subject of such woful neglect and ill treatment?

Nothing is ever said about being treated like a horse, a cow, or an elephant. No: the Dog, the *only* disinterested and faithful friend of man, is *alone* the fitting symbol of degradation and outlawry; the butt and by-word of all nations, kindreds and tongues.

What apology, then, shall be demanded of the honest, educated, philanthropic TIGER, for introducing himself to the public as the champion and defender of canine rights?

What, if a penalty were imposed on the *master* for neglecting the education of his dog! Few, indeed, would escape punishment. What is *man*, when left to the unrestricted indulgence of his natural perverseness? Who would be seen in his company, or who would meet him in the dark? How, then, shall untutored Doghood befit the society of enlightened Humanity?

TIGER presents to our notice many happy illustrations of superior talents and refinement, hoping that these striking examples of fidelity and usefulness may tend to ameliorate the condition of his outcast brethren.

His narrative is plain, straight-forward and truthful; and he no doubt flatters himself it may prove both amusing and instructive, convincing his readers (through his own personal experience, confirmed by many of his contemporaries) that they will be amply rewarded for every leisure moment which may be devoted to the development of those reasoning faculties which he himself undoubtedly possessed.

DOGO-GRAPHY.

CHAPTER I.

TIGER'S FATHER.

My name is "TIGER." How far I may have merited this ferocious title, those who peruse my biography will be the fittest to determine. Not to boast of my noble deeds do I introduce myself to the public; but it strikes me it is indeed high time that one of our *own* race should spring up in our defense, to enlighten our superiors as to our ideas, notions, capacities, and powers. However, before I begin to expatiate on my own virtues and failings, it is of no slight importance to my narrative, that I should give you some information as to my origin, descent, and pedigree. I am not a little proud of my blood-relations; my father and mother especially, and (they say) several of my ancestors, having been the heroes of many a sanguinary conflict.

My father's name was "Don," and he died with this distinguished title engraven on the golden collar with which he was awarded after his last glorious victory at the far-famed battle of Gloster. He had been the lucky recipient of many valuable premiums in consideration of his valor—was never known to turn his back on an enemy, having been declared the winner of every battle he fought. He was a pure bred bull-dog, white as snow, with the exception of his nose and the inside of his mouth, which were perfectly black; his weight was about forty pounds, (vulgarly called his *fighting weight;*) his limbs were well defined and beautifully proportioned. His expression was serious and determined, bold yet unobtrusive. He scorned to quarrel with an ignoble foe, and looked disdainfully on all miniature specimens of canine impudence; but he either could or would not overlook a serious insult from any of his class without an immediate apology. I have heard that he once pitched a little noisy, insolent cur off a bridge into the river, considering him too mean for the ordinary method of chastisement. He retired from his military career several years previous to his demise, devoting himself solely to carnal and vegetable pursuits. Towards the last, his sight becoming dim and his hearing dull, he took but little interest in what was passing around him, and might generally be found either basking in the sun or snoring by the fire; yet he was so well known as the guardian of the night, that none, even at this advanced period of his glorious career, ever ventured to encroach on the grounds he had been wont to protect. No: Don was there: when he spoke he meant, "Remember me!"

Unfortunately, we who happen to show any signs of the bull-dog breed in our physiognomy are set down as quarrelsome, ill-tempered, and snarlish; just as though we wanted to be fighting and biting everybody and everything that crossed our path. It is true, we are generally of rather a haughty, vindictive turn of mind; but because we are courageous and unflinching, and man delights in prostituting our valor to satisfy his cruel and mercenary appetites, are we to be the by-word of ferocity and treachery? It is only because we are despised, that we render ourselves despicable; many of us being never introduced into society at all, which naturally makes us sullen, morose, and sulky. Give us only the advantages of a common Newfoundland or even Scotch-terrier-education, and (my word for it) we will be as sociable as a King Charley spaniel, or a poodle.

CHAPTER II.

TIGER INTRODUCES US TO HIS MOTHER.

But my pedigree is as yet incomplete, and I doubt not you must be exceedingly anxious to learn something about my mother. Her talents differed widely from those of my father: she was quite of another complexion, far inferior in size, and of a totally different caste. She was considered a perfect specimen of a Scotch terrier, being more properly termed a fox-terrier; and well was she worthy of the name. His Lordship of D—— thought more of his favorite "Vixen," than of his whole pack of splendid fox-hounds. She was considered very handsome of her kind, about twelve pounds weight, rather short in the leg, of a sandy complexion, very rough hair, with a pair of black, sparkling eyes, shining through her whiskery phiz like two magic lanterns. She was naturally of a mild, winning disposition, which was no doubt greatly improved by education and society. She was allowed the run of the whole hunting establishment; and as she had the strongest antipathy to all kinds of vermin, neither rat, mouse, skunk, nor weasel dared to venture within the limits of her range. She was on intimate terms with every steed in those extensive and magnificent stables, and there was not a horse in the whole stud, but would have lost his supper rather than set a foot on her. She also took her daily promenades among the whole pack of fox-hounds, visited the isolated abodes of Newfoundlands, pointers, setters, etc. when rare indeed was it that she met with the slightest insult. She might often be seen romping with the whole pack, and the moment any of the less educated showed the least rudeness, a simple turn of my mother's mustachoed lips would command respect. T'was a fine sight, indeed, to see her, in company with a splendid pack of fox-hounds, all aroused for action at early dawn. How they danced, and sprung, and played, and fondled around my poor mother, in testimony of their respect, whilst, no doubt, they would occasionally whisper to her the absolute necessity of her presence in the anticipated hunt. In fact, my mother always *did* accompany them, as her services were required to dislodge old Renard, should he have taken to earth through neglect of the stoppers, whose business it was to close all the fox-holes the day previous to the chase. Many a hard struggle has she had in those dark recesses; but her courage never forsook her. When Renard was there she would make a bold dash, perhaps some twenty or thirty feet under-ground, face the polished ivories of the pugnacious fox, and, in spite of his despairing efforts, drag him forth inch by inch; after which, he was allowed a respectable start and the chase was continued.

My mother presented a rather forlorn appearance after these bloody encounters, but she never relaxed her hold till her adversary was delivered to safe keeping. The more she was punished, the more delighted did she seem with her victory; and, after shaking her wiry self, would cheerfully and merrily resume the chase, anxious and greedy for a second conflict. In one of these subterraneous skirmishes she was near losing her life: an old dog-fox, twice her own weight, was determined not to be dislodged, and *did* maintain his ground, to the cost of his life; indeed, my mother was so completely exhausted, as to lay almost lifeless by his side. Some minutes after, she was dug out, most dreadfully lacerated and with the loss of an eye. Three such cheers the woods never echoed before, as were then shouted over the vanquished form of her lifeless foe. Although disappointment at the wind-up of the day's sport seemed to pervade the white breeches and scarlet coats of the anxious hunters, yet the glorious little Vixen was the admiration of all, and the subject of many a merry toast. All admired her daring, praised her courage, and extolled her endurance and tenacity. She was also useful in stirring the fox out of thick cover where a hound could not enter, being often the first to announce the prelude to a good day's sport.

CHAPTER III.

TIGER'S BIRTH-PLACE AND BRETHREN.

I must now give you a second introduction to myself. Again I say my name is Tiger. I was born, pupped, or whelped, (just as you please,) in one of the first stables of England, where huntsmen and whippers-in, grooms and stablemen delighted to congregate: also dukes, lords and gentry often stalked around there; and I assure you *we* attracted the attention of all visitors—that is to say, myself and my little brothers and sisters, as we all frolicked together among the horses. But I suppose *I* was more noticed than the rest of the family, from my being entirely white, whilst *they* were of the exact shade of my mother; in fact, the expression of all beholders, on their first seeing me, was, "Dear me! how exactly like his father!" I was white and smooth, with full black eyes and round head; whilst my brethren were all yellow and rough, weasel-eyed, and whiskery. Some of the knowing ones assert that we of the same family are often not of the same paternal origin, which I firmly deny, although I must confess our mothers are strangely fickle in their amorous propensities at certain periods of their history; yet I insist on it, not a single female of our tribe has ever produced a progeny that could boast of a duplicate sire.

CHAPTER IV.

TIGER TORN FROM HIS MOTHER.—HIS FIRST TRIALS.

One morning, an old acquaintance and pot-companion of one of the stablemen dropped in, and insisted on lining one of his pockets with *me*. The stableman gave him a point-blank refusal, telling him I was his lordship's favorite, and the only one of that color; that I should be missed immediately; but that if he must have one, to take one of the others, etc. Before he had concluded his speech, however, I was safely ensconced in my new master's coat-tail pocket, and traveling at about ten knots an hour, with the stableman after me. But he never overtook us: had he succeeded in so doing, whatever might have been my joys and sorrows through life, it is very improbable that I should have to record any of the scenes on which I involuntarily entered on that eventful day.

The morning after my disappearance, there was a general *hue-and-cry* throughout the whole establishment: every one was called to account, every nook and corner was searched; but all denied any knowledge of my whereabouts or of what might have become of me. It was at last concluded by all, (with the exception of the stableman, who had seen me triumphantly borne away,) that I had been ignominiously swallowed by two half-grown greyhounds who chanced to be unkenneled, and were seen in the stable on the day of my disappearance. On arriving at his cottage, Dick Marks took me by the leg and dragged me out of his pocket. The first test he put me to, was swinging me round by the ears, then by the tail; then he would hold me up by one leg, then by the other, just to see if I was (what he called) *game*. I can't say I was *particularly* delighted with his masterly ideas, and in my own peculiar canine brogue I addressed him to that effect, which only excited him to teaze me the more. He took me to his favorite pot-house in the evening, when the whole company amused themselves with pulling my ears and tail, which I certainly resented to the best of my ability, causing them all to decide that I should made a *good 'un*. I was certainly very dissatisfied with the peculiar method they had of testing my natural abilities; but 't was not till my protector thrust me into a dark coal-hole at night, previous to his returning drunk to bed, that I felt all the horrors of my situation. I whined, fretted, barked, howled, and yelled, hoping that perchance some one might come to my relief;

and every time I stopped to catch my breath, I thought of my mother and my little brothers and sisters, and of the comfortable home from which I had been so ruthlessly torn. At last I heard, as I thought, somebody coming to my release, when in pounced my infuriated lord, and lashed me to such a degree that both of us concluded it was our last meeting. I was too sore to think of making any more noise that night; in any case, I rather think I should have been very cautious in the experiment, for fear of a second visit. For all he had dealt so roughly with me, I really was delighted to see him in the morning, and grateful for the scanty allowance of bread which he gave to me. I felt, indeed, that he was the only friend I had in the world. It may seem strange, but I never harbored the least resentment towards him, and passed the following nights as quietly as possible, lest I might disturb his repose, or perchance incline him to make a second descent on me. One of his favorite amusements was throwing me at the cat; and it tickled him amazingly to see her scratch my face and spit on me, whilst he boasted how courageously I resented her insults. I hadn't the least idea of interfering with her myself; but when I found she treated me in that abrupt, unladylike manner, I handled (or rather toothed) her accordingly, and invariably succeeded in putting her to flight. I afterwards noticed how cautious she was to keep out of my way, little as I felt disposed to annoy her without provocation.

CHAPTER V.

TIGER IS SOLD FOR EIGHTEEN-PENCE.

But one fine morning, when Dick Marks' pockets were as empty as a mummy's, and his throat drier than a lime-basket, he took me in his arms, determined (as he thought for his stomach's sake) to have a week's spree out of me.

Finding no one on the king's highway who appeared to second his ideas as to price, he ventured to ring at the gate of a gentleman's mansion. Out comes the footman. "Will you please to ask master if he do want to buy a nice dog?" says Dick. But the footman answered him by saying, "I'm sure my master don't want to buy any fighting dogs;" and *bang* went the gate in Dick's face and mine, making him grumble and me growl. But Dick Marks was so dry, so very dry, that he was not to be easily daunted, and rang the bell a second time, determined to deliver an oration on my noble pedigree, my precocious instinct and sagacity, my wonderful snapping, growling, and cat-shaking propensities, and to expatiate on the emptiness of his pockets, the dryness of his throat, and the extraordinary aversion of his better-half to the whole canine fraternity. He had scarcely withdrawn his hand from the bell, when the gate was opened by the young master, who was immediately attracted by my fair complexion, round head, and large black eyes. He asked Dick a hundred questions concerning me, and, according to the account Mr. Richard Marks gave of me, you might have valued me at least at a hundred pounds. With it all, the young squire believed only *just enough* of it to offer eighteen-pence for me, which Dick, after traveling shilling by shilling from two guineas downwards, (his throat growing drier as he spoke,) half willingly consented to accept. I need scarcely mention, that previous to his retiring to his nocturnal dormitory, my *spirit* (to the tune of eighteen-pence) had passed down Mr. Richard Marks' unquenchable throat.

CHAPTER VI.

TIGER'S FIRST ADVENTURE WITH A KING CHARLES SPANIEL.—GETS INTO DISGRACE, AND IS PUT OUT TO BOARD.

But now I am a gentleman's dog, and my new master seemed highly delighted with me, although he was loth to believe a tithe of what he was obliged to hear of me: he nevertheless thought he might realize a little sport by bringing me in contact with his mother's favorite King Charles spaniel, who was about six months old and much larger than myself; besides, I was only in the ninth week of my pilgrimage. Accordingly, he took us both by the back of the neck, and began by rubbing our noses together, which you may readily presume was particularly annoying to us both. Charley's monster eyes rolled about in all directions: his quivering lip spake volumes of defiance: his teeth fairly chattered with rage. As to my own private feelings, they might be far more easily imagined than described. I growled and bit; he grumbled and snapped. On the young gent's perceiving that we were in a high state of honorable excitement, he put us on the ground, to decide, by a *dental* demonstration, whether or not I was as heroic as I had been represented. No sooner were we on *terra-firma*, than I grasped my adversary by the throat and began shaking him most furiously, for I really felt as though I had lost all government of myself. My adversary soon signified his perfect willingness to relinquish the combat, but I could admit of no apology, and could have killed him with pleasure. He used his utmost to escape me; but in his flight I clung fast to him, and did not relinquish my hold till I positively began to think he was carrying me out of the bounds of reason. I then let him go and gave up the pursuit, contenting myself by noticing the direction he took and the unmusical sounds he uttered, as he hastily retreated toward the back kitchen-door.

During this short, but to me novel encounter, my master

was wonderfully delighted, clapping his hands and straining his ribs with laughter. He had but just taken me in his arms, was patting and praising me up, and christening me "Tiger," when his mother presented herself, reprimanding her son in unmeasured terms for his cruelty, and utterly condemning me as one of the most despicable, plebeian brutes in all creation; whilst she discanted on the intrinsic merits, the prominent virtues, and extraordinary beauty of her cowardly Charley. She even threatened my life; but the cause of her displeasure so thoroughly convinced my master of my real merit, that he determined on raising me for his own private companion. An old woman, who chanced to be weeding the flower-beds, had straightened her back to listen to the angry intonations of the offended lady, and on the latter's retiring, advised my new protector to send me away as quickly as possible, kindly volunteering to take charge of me herself for the reasonable sum of one shilling per week. The offer was immediately accepted, on condition that I should be brought over to the house every Saturday for inspection.

CHAPTER VII.

TIGER'S NEW MISTRESS.—INTRODUCTION TO HER BOARDERS.—CHARACTERISTICS OF TRIPEY AND HER HUSBAND SAM.

The old lady of whom I am now speaking, was one of the oddest, drollest, queerest, funniest dames in all creation; and I had not long resided under her roof before I discovered it. She often observed how fond she was of *dumb critters*, and my experience confirmed the fact. She lived in a very little, small, old, thatched cottage, with one room on the ground-floor, with a garret overhead. There were to be no more like her, as she had never been blessed with any offsets. She always declared she was glad of it, and I believe I had reason to be so too. I have no doubt she would have thought less about us *dumb critters*, had she any bantlings of her own; though she certainly would have made an excellent mother, if I may judge from the order and obedience which reigned in her adopted family. I was wonderfully startled, however, when she first introduced me to her boarders. No sooner had she opened the door, than the monkey chattered, the dog barked, the cat mewed, the magpie screamed, the blackbird whistled, and Sam (her husband) grumbled. But the moment she spoke, they *all* hushed. Never shall I forget how they eyed me as I passed the door-sill. Truffle, a low, long-backed, nasty, little blear-eyed mongrel of a turnspit poodle Scotch terrier, looked unutterable things at me. He walked backwards and forwards, at a short distance from me, with an air of cowardly defiance; which, on my perceiving, caused me to stiffen myself up a little, presuming that he might perhaps be meditating an attack on me; but the old lady (nicknamed Tripey) immediately ordered Truffle to his bed, which he obeyed instantaneously. When I first saw him bolt, I thought he was afraid of me: I was just starting after him, but Tripey gave me a cut with the whip, accompanied by a suitable reprimand. I don't know how it was, but I felt as though I was bound to obey her. Poor Tom, the cat, bristled himself up into a semicircle, every hair of him threatening to fly off into infinite space. The magpie and blackbird both looked down on me with a kind of affrighted astonishment, while I stood wondering at their taking so much notice of me, when I thought so little about them. Nevertheless, the monkey (I must say) rather alarmed me: he jumped, sprung, and danced, making the most awful grimaces at me: but did'nt he (Johnny, the monkey,) raise a scream when he felt the unwelcome embrace of Tripey's whip! I really do believe he thought it was my fault, for he kept slyly peeping around at me through his fingers, straining his eyes in all directions, looking alternately at his feet and tail, at me and old Tripey, though not daring to make any further advances.

I soon had a snug little corner allotted to me, where the old lady presumed Johnny could not reach me. I complained dreadfully at first about being tied up with a collar on my neck, and undertook to be restive, discontented, and grumbling; but when I found the old lady would allow of no disturbance in the house, I soon became perfectly quiet and contented. Sam (her husband) was the very essence of laziness and discontent. It is true, he worked *sometimes*, but never when he had anything to eat. He would toil hard for twelve hours to earn flour for three days, which he would make into a dumpling and boil, invariably staying home till it was all consumed. Sam and his wife Tripey were never known to meal together at the same table or to eat of the same loaf; nor were they ever heard to agree on any subject whatever. The idols of the one were sure to be the antipathies of the other. Sam liked victuals and indolence, Tripey was wedded to liquor and hard work; Sam spoke but little, and that very slowly; Tripey chattered incessantly as fast as a horse could gallop. In fine, Tripey was devotedly fond of *dumb critters*, while Sam hated the sight of us all. He would sometimes give me a sly kick, if I chanced to brush by him, when Tripey threatened to deprive him of the skimmings of the pot in which the tripe was boiled, thereby causing him to treat us all with comparative civility in her presence.

CHAPTER VIII.

TIGER GREATLY ANNOYED AND IRRITATED BY JOHNNY, THE MONKEY. BECOMES INTIMATE WITH DOG TRUFFLE, AND TOM, THE CAT.

The old lady was often absent the whole day; when Sam enjoyed himself at home, if there happened to be any of his *dump* unconsumed. On these occasions we often began raising a row, as soon as Tripey's back was turned, especially Johnny, who took every opportunity of annoying *me*, and I found to my sorrow that he was longer in the reach than either she or I had anticipated or desired. For a long time I got no rest during her absence. He no sooner saw me curled up comfortably, than he would slyly creep along and give me a sharp pull by the tail or a smart pinch in the ear, and before I could look round, he was quietly seated on his stool, defiantly grinning at me. True, I always showed him my teeth, challenging him to face me in open combat; but he invariably declined the honor, preferring, no doubt, the sport of worrying me, without the risk of retaliation. Although we were often brought in contact together on professional business, when, of course, we were bound to appear on friendly terms, I never could forgive him; for, independent of his almost daily annoyances, he took every opportunity of showing his *apish* superiority over me: he would even make faces at me in company, and when I was offered any refreshment, would rudely snatch it from me, without even giving me an opportunity of testing its merits. On such occasions I was made the laughing-stock of the whole company, causing me to feel very insignificant; and although I never failed to show my resentment, my mistress kept me in check; I was consequently bound to pocket the affront.

Truffle I certainly began soon to be quite partial to, as we were occasionally allowed to take short rambles together, when he always treated me with the greatest respect: we played together in perfect good humor—exercised ourselves in sham fights, always standing up in our mutual defence, should either of us chance to be insulted. I have often thought how selfish we are toward our own race, and how self-denying toward our protectors. For instance: partial as I was to Truffle, I never felt inclined to offer him anything I could eat myself: on the contrary, I sometimes threatened him with my dire resentment, when he refused to relinquish any choice morsel he might have discovered. He seldom, indeed, wanted asking a second time, after having experienced the force of my arguments, although he generally yielded with considerable reluctance. On the other hand, I felt as though I could sacrifice anything for my protectress, and have left the choicest dinner to accompany her in her travels.

At first I felt very anxious to have a set-to with the cat, but Tom gradually endeared himself to my affections; he not only never offered to molest me, but would even lie down by my side, appearing to hold me in the highest estimation; so that we shortly became so familiar that he would even take possession of my bed; and so pleased was I with the confidence he reposed in me, that I never once offered to disturb him. He pushed his intimacy still further, and would curl himself upon me and snore in my face for hours at a time. He thus kept me (and I suppose himself) delightfully warm, and I have often postponed my movements rather than disturb his repose. In spite of this intimacy, I was far from being a friend to the feline race, although I have found some honorable exceptions to their faithless, spit-fire, sneaking characteristics. But Johnny was an awful scourge to us both, even Tripey herself often suffering from his mischievous antics. If she only turned her back to go an errand, master Johnny would sometimes collect all the soot he could reach and stir it carefully into her tripe-pot, and on her return, would look as innocent as a sheep-stealer. I have really been greatly surprised he should repeat the operation, as I never knew him escape with a sound belt. But "mischief is bound up in the heart of a" monkey. Notwithstanding, I always thought if I only had a fair chance, I could shake it out of him.

CHAPTER IX.

TIGER'S EARLY LESSONS WITH THE CAT, MONKEY, AND TRUFFLE.

Old Tripey sometimes took out Johnny Truffle and me to the neighboring pot-houses, in the following marching order: Tom the cat was seated on one of her shoulders, Johnny on the other, while Truffle and I kept in the rear. When she said "*In!*" neither of us dared to advance; we severally had tried the game on various occasions, when, if Tripey had failed to notice our errant steps, that confounded monkey would surely advise her of them. The old lady used but little severity with us; but somehow or other we all seemed fascinated to her commands, and seldom committed any gross act of disobedience. She had taught me to lie down on my back perfectly motionless; but I confess I was previously subjected to sundry cracks of her leather whip, as she scolded and corrected me every time I moved or growled. I never dared even to open my eyes without her distinct command, and was bound tacitly to submit to whatever insults might be heaped upon me. I could have borne them all with comparative patience and canine submission, but to be dragged about the room by a *monkey*, with a cat on his back, while Truffle amused himself barking at us, irritated my feelings to that degree, that I was bent on revenge, should ever a favorable opportunity present itself.

The old lady would get so awfully intoxicated, especially when Johnny was lucky with his favorite sixpenny trick, that (with the exception of Tom) we have often reposed the whole night in the ditch. Although our washing and lodging were gratis, master Thomas invariably bolted home—I presume in hopes of getting a fair chance at the tripe in his mistress' absence. I believe that scoundrel Johnny would have cleared out too, but he was always buckled fast on to Tripey's wrist, and did'nt forget to show his teeth when any-one came near her. Not that I imagine he cared a single nut about *her*, but he was afraid of his own jacket. I don't like boasting, but I really fancy Truffle and I were far more sincere and less selfish than he was; for I'm sure nothing could have tempted either of us to leave her for a moment, and more than once we have fought like tigers in her defence. He was cunning enough, (I say it to my sorrow,) but I doubt whether he had a spark of sincerity about him. His sixpenny-trick was this: Tripey announced that the best trick of all was the sixpenny-trick, which Johnny could only perform with sixpences. When a sixpence was given him, he invariably put it in his pouch, (or receiving stomach,) but he had been taught, at the peril of his life, not to eject anything without her orders. In this way he would sometimes receive several sixpences; but none were ever disgorged except to herself, although she feigned to threaten him, and *did* actually deal him out a few cracks to make her own case good. But Johnny knew his work too well, and was taught only to *shell out* at one particular command, which was never given in public. Tom had'nt much sense, except to take care of himself. He cared more about the house than the tenant; though I suspect Tripey thought more of him than she did of us, as I often observed he got most of the little delicate bits, and had the warmest post in the chimney-corner. On our return from such a nocturnal adventure as that to which I have just alluded, Tom was generally screwed up against the door outside, as Sam never troubled his head about who was in or who was out. He, however, generally abused *us* without reserve on our return; to which our good mistress invariably responded with usurious interest, seldom forgetting to add her threat of depriving him of the skimmings of the tripe pot. This privilege was granted only on condition of his taking care of the family in her absence, but depended mostly on his general deportment, as she often employed him to do little errands, which, when not executed with due precision, elicited a variety of threats, which she occasionally stamped on his organs of mastication.

CHAPTER X.

TRIPEY'S PECULIAR METHOD OF INSTRUCTING HER PUPILS.

Tripey was always teaching us something or other, and whilst Sam was snoring over his dumpling, she scarcely ever ceased to address us, both individually and collectively;

particularly the magpie and blackbird, who seldom appeared to take much notice of her incessant jabber. They *did* profit wonderfully, though, by her nightly lessons, as they repeated portions of them at early dawn; in fact, they *had* to do their best before their breakfasts were served out to them. The magpie was a far apter scholar than the blackbird, as far as conversation was concerned. They say blackbirds are seldom known to say much, but this fellow said a good many funny things (I suppose:) I didn't understand much of it, but t'was so near like the old lady's clatter, that he often deceived both Truffle and me. She had a wonderful method of instructing *me*—*I* never could get a mouthful without doing something for it. How quick I learned to jump through a hoop, when there was a nice bit of tripe on the other side of it! At first I tried to go round, but I found no tripe that way; consequently, I had to go through. Unfortunately, I have had to travel the same road a thousand times for nothing, as when she knew what I *could* do, there was no *backing out* with *her*. Nevertheless, she would not allow me to perform in public without *our* being paid beforehand, and with strangers I invariably expected a little refreshment in advance. Before I was nine months old, I could sit up and stand up, could dance, jump, be very lively or very dead, go little errands, fetch and carry, etc.; in fact, if I could only have spoken, I could have given lessons in manners to more than half the so-called human beings who pelted me in the streets.

CHAPTER XI.

TIGER RESTORED TO HIS MASTER.—SORROWFUL PARTING FROM TRIPEY, ETC.

During the interval of events, some of which I have related, I was presented weekly to my young master, who was delighted with my progress, in testimony of which he had presented my tutoress with many an extra shilling. Indeed, even his once-offended mother began to take great notice of me: her former opinions of my *horrid* temper and loaferish aspect gradually faded away, and I was even made the subject of drawing-room conversations. It was at last agreed by all parties that I should be received at home, on condition that I should be kept *out of doors*. I was then about eleven months old, and began to have a pretty good opinion of myself, and by the respectful manner in which I was treated by the majority of common bone-grubbers, I continued to acquire confidence. It was with the greatest reluctance that Tripey consented to give me up, and the briny tear trickled down her wrinkled phiz as she saw me chained up in the coach-house. She shook hands with me, kissed me, hugged me, loaded me with blessings and good advice, and crowned her good wishes by giving me a whole half-pound of tripe on a skewer. My feelings were such, when she closed the door on me, that I could not refrain from weeping; on hearing which, she re-entered and endeavored to console me; but as the tripe lay untouched, she gave it as her decided opinion that I never could possibly survive the separation. But her grief was somewhat alleviated when my young master presented her with half a sovereign, accompanied with the permission to visit me whenever she pleased. That night I really felt bereaved, and if I could have escaped by any means I should have made a quick passage home. I tried to slip my head through the collar, till I found all my efforts were vain; next I tugged at the chain, then tried to bite it off. Finding that all my exertions were fruitless, I concluded to curl myself up in my bed and resign myself to my fate. I passed the night in sorrowfully meditating on Tripey and Truffle, Johnny and Tom, the magpie and blackbird. I heard all sorts of strange noises that night, but heeded them not, being too deeply immersed in my own troubles. I had left my supper untouched; and though in the morning I felt a strong inclination for my breakfast, my heart went against it, my every hope being centred in effecting my escape.

CHAPTER XII.

TIGER'S EARS ARE CUT OFF.—BECOMES FRIENDLY WITH CHARLEY.

The rays of the morning sun had already brightened my hopes, when, to my great joy, the coach-house door was opened, and my young master entered, with the gardener and a stranger. The former immediately released me, and I began scampering around in high spirits, expecting a favorable opportunity of a speedy retreat to my late domicil. But the stranger kindly called me to himself, taking me up *very affectionately*, when suddenly I found myself made fast by the head and throat by the gardener, while the strange ruffian coolly cut off both my ears. It was a pretty severe operation, but I didn't care so much about the cutting, as the idea of being jammed up and half choked to death: indeed, I really supposed they intended to murder me, and I struggled for my life; but they had me too fast, and succeeded in *cropping* me, as they called it. When I found that was all they were going to inflict on me, I felt quite relieved and cared but little about it, after having had (as I imagined) such a narrow escape of my life. But they said 't was done *first-rate*, and that I looked fifty pounds better. Although it was to me such a frightful operation, I have since benefited by it in a hundred skirmishes, in which I'm sure my ears would have been awfully lacerated and disfigured; besides, it gave me a better chance of seizing my opponents, by decreasing their chance of holding me. On the same afternoon of the operation the old woman came to see me, and her lamentations over me were far louder and longer than my own. She *swore* I should not stop there a moment longer; that my tail would come off next, and that soon there wouldn't be a morsel of me left. She took some fat off the tripe she carried in her basket and rubbed it on my ears, at the same time praising me up, and heaping anathemas on my murderers, as she called them; after which she toddled out of the gate, and I after her, forgetting the soreness of my ears. But my young master immediately ordered her to bring me back; to which she at last assented, after exacting a faithful promise that my ears should never be cut off again. In a few days I felt perfectly well, beginning to consider myself at home, especially as the old lady was so constant in her visits. I had a good dinner every day, besides sundry choice morsels, and was allowed the run of the whole premises. Every one seemed to take notice of me, and even the good lady of the house was charmed to see me gamboling with her favorite Charley, who, I must admit, obeyed my orders far more implicitly than hers. When *I* called him he obeyed instantaneously, and my commands of dismissal were attended to with equal promptness; but I have heard *her* call him a dozen times, and all the response he made was a *don't-carish* kind of a Charley grin, and away he went. When she bid him go in the house, he generally slunk back a *little*, but seldom obeyed to the letter. I had been taught better. When Tripey said, "Go!" 't was "*Go;*" and when she said, "*Come!*" there was no saying "Nay." Habit to me had become second nature, and I doubt not that my early instructions were the means of prolonging my existence and contributing greatly to my means of enjoyment. I have often pitied those poor, contemptible, uneducated curs, dragging their scanty sustenance from the gutter or the ash-heap, the by-word of every ragged urchin, and (from constantly being imposed on) flying from their own shadows. I am quite of Shakspeare's opinion—

> **"I'd rather be a dog,**
> **"And bay the moon."**

CHAPTER XIII.

GRADUAL DEVELOPMENT OF TIGER'S SAGACITY AND DISCERNMENT.

I soon became a general favorite, and as to my young master, he seldom dreamed of going out without me: I became his constant companion. When I chanced not to be with him, the first inquiry was, "Where's Tiger?" As I gradually became older and wiser, I afforded great amusement wherever I went, by the superior developments of my absolute reasoning propensities. I could discern at a glance whether my company was desirable or not, and never ventured to intrude where I had reason to presume I might be unwelcome. I have often remarked that the attention of a whole company was lavished on me, while a simple shake of the hand was all that fell to my master's share. No society was considered too select, no house too clean, and no carpet too fine for me. It is true, I had been taught to wipe my feet perfectly clean, previous to advancing into any respectable dwelling, and was too refined in my manners to commit any kind of nuisance in a proscribed locality. I was the subject of many wagers concerning my varied performances, both instinctive, instructive, scientific, and pugnacious. I could select from a thousand bushels the apple which my master had touched; could jump through a straw without touching it, while my master held both ends between his fingers; could kill more rats in the same number of minutes than any other dog in the country; while a hundred other convincing proofs of canine educational development endeared me to a large circle of a higher order of acquaintances. But it was only in my master's presence that I considered myself entitled to form any new *human* acquaintance, and I looked suspiciously on every one to whom I had only had a passing introduction. As I began to be more aristocratic in my ideas, I imagined that no sneaking, itinerant heap of rags and filth ought to be tolerated on our premises; and although I was particular in ascertaining of all visitors whether they came on legitimate business, and never allowed them to be out of my sight till one of the household presented himself, I discerned something so peculiar in the strange, unbusiness-like visits of these inquisitive, peeping marauders, that I at length concluded to contest their very passage to the kitchen-door. I did not wish to be severe with them, but was in the habit of simply ordering them off, when I was generally obeyed, although several times I have seen fit to resort to forcible means of ejectment when remonstrance had proved unavailing.

CHAPTER XIV.

OLD SAM SELLS TIGER FOR TWO SHILLINGS.—TIGER IS TAKEN TO BRISTOL, AND FIGHTS THE RENOWNED STUMP-TAILED BULL-DOG, "GRAB."

It was now several months since Tripey had restored me to my young master; since which, although she visited me so often, Sam had never once made his appearance. But one morning I chanced to be out alone, taking a little airing in the road, when Sam made his appearance in the distance. I felt so delighted, that I scampered off to meet him. He appeared to receive me very cordially, patting and flattering me, and even offered me a small piece of dry dumpling, which he extracted from his pantaloon pocket. Although I was not hungry enough to avail myself of his *unaccustomed* liberality, I trust I did not feel ungrateful for his self-denial. At that moment a rag-merchant chanced to be passing with his wagon, and cast his eyes on me, as I was rejoicing over my old acquaintance. A short parley ensued, and in less than two minutes Sam had ignominiously bargained me away to him for the paltry sum of two shillings. I was hastily chained fast under his wagon, and suddenly discovered that I was traveling, at about seven miles an hour, on the high road to Bristol, about thirty miles distant. I pulled and dragged, and looked all round for help, but to no purpose; the collar was too tight, the chain was too strong, and I found I was only hurting myself without any prospect of escape; so I coolly kept pace with the horse and away we went. On arriving at our destination I was made fast in the yard, with a bare empty barrel for a bed, and a cramped-up range of about two feet. I tried in vain to escape, but felt resolved to await patiently the first opportunity of flight. I had only a hard crust or two for my supper that night, but being almost ravenous after my long journey, I bolted them with avidity. On the following morning I was led about on the chain, and offered for sale. Several bids were made for me, but Tom Lincoln set me at a pretty high figure, and none of his sporting friends being accustomed to pay over five shillings for a fighting dog, unless his *metal* had been positively put to the test, he could discover no immediate probability of converting me into cash. He therefore offered to fight me against *anything* of my weight for all the money he could raise, which turned out to be exactly fourteen shillings and ninepence halfpenny. A subscription was shortly raised among his companions to match me, and in less than half an hour, a big-headed brindle, stump-tailed bull-dog was introduced to us. We were immediately surrounded by a ragged set of horrid-looking loafers, whooping, yelling, and swearing. A ring was formed. Tom Lincoln took off my chain and collar and held me in his arms, while Jim Sykes held up my stump-tailed adversary (the renowned "Grab") in the same tender, affectionate way. Grab commenced by making horrid, unintellectual grimaces at me, growling and showing his teeth in the most daring manner. I was satisfied I had never injured him in any way, and felt astounded to think that, without the least provocation, he should thus furiously threaten me: I concluded by presuming that some evil-disposed person or persons had poisoned his mind against me in some way or other. Be the cause what it may, as he evidently threatened me with personal violence, I placed myself on the defensive, determined, in case of an assault, to fight to the last gasp.

The whole host of fancy gentlemen were delighted at our distorted countenances: pints, quarts, gallons, sixpences, and shillings were freely staked on both of us. Down we were put, face to face, Tom Lincoln *handling* me, and Dick Sykes seconding Grab. We were both let go at once. Grab seized me first by the ear, and the way he gnawed and shook, mumbled and thumped me, would have broken poor old Tripey's heart. "Another quart on Grab!" "Sixpence more on Grab!" "Go it Grab—well done Grab—shake him Grab!" "*Hany* more Tigers on *'and*, Tom?" "*Ee'll* soon be a *goner!* Take hoff your dog, Tom! What's the use o' 'avin on 'im killed? He's a pretty dog enough; some fool may gin ye a crown for'n yet." Although I must confess I by no means relished this so-called "capital sport," I never once whimpered or *gave tongue*, but awaited only my chance of retaliation; in fact, I was so completely *in for it*, that I would absolutely have preferred death to a surrender. After a few minutes Grab let go his hold, when I immediately seized him by the foreleg, and could fairly hear it crack, crack, crack, as I repeated my efforts at grinding it up. However, as I felt inclined to punish him still more severely, I loosened him, with the intention of attacking a more vital spot, when Grab again fastened me by the back of the neck, mawling me in the same way as before; but I scarcely heeded it now, and even felt willing to die, rather than yield an inch. He loosened me again, upon which I seized him by the throat, and felt determined to make an end of him. I soon succeeded in getting him down flat on his back, after which I had it all my own way. As I gradually worked my passage to his windpipe, while his eyes protruded from their sockets and his blackened tongue lolled motionless between his teeth, Tom Lincoln's voice was heard victoriously shouting, "Well done, Tiger! kill him, Tiger! at him again, Tiger!"

CHAPTER XV.

TIGER'S REFLECTIONS AFTER HIS VICTORY.—IS COMPELLED TO SLAUGHTER A TOM-CAT.

Grab was dead, and I, inoffensive Tiger, had killed him. I might have met him a hundred times in the street, and not an unkind sound would have tainted our muzzles; a canine sniff, or a significant raise of the understanding, would probably have terminated the interview. Thousands of us are daily traveling the streets and roaming the fields, and the most unenlightened quadruped among us, seldom, if ever, infringes on the acknowledged rights even of uncivilized dogdom; but when abused, irritated, and excited, he is a despicable cur indeed who would shrink from demanding an apology, or screen his pelt by an ignoble flight. I never felt really debased but once, and I was worthy of it: I am well nigh ashamed to own it; but I was then young and inexperienced, and learned a very important lesson—not to place confidence in those with whom I was unacquainted. I felt inclined to enjoy a little sport with a few romping juveniles, when they regaled me with a second-or third-hand teakettle, and having tightly fastened it to my extremity, they entreated me to retire to my domicil with the utmost speed, while stones and other missiles greeted me, as I hastened to obey their commands.

On the night of my victory, I was the main topic of conversation among all the crownless hats and ragged elbows of the enlightened neighborhood where I had achieved my first victory. Tom Lincoln was so elated with his extra fourteen shillings and ninepence-halfpenny which he had won on me, that he offered to find backers to match me again for fifty pounds. He then offered to bet half a sovereign that I would kill a cat in two minutes—yes, any cat they liked to bring against me. The bet was accepted, and an enormous tom-cat was soon procured. Tom Lincoln commenced this glorious piece of fun by making the cat spit on my face and scratch my nose, which, of course, aggravated me beyond all bearing. He then took off my collar and threw the cat right at me. Tom, naturally enough, began sticking his claws into me, which maddened me to that degree, that I immediately seized him across the loins and did not release my hold till I witnessed his last gasp. It was decided that I had finished off Master Thomas in the short space of eighty seconds. Tom Lincoln now thought his fortune made, and agreed that I should be ready at the "Boar and Whistle" on the morrow evening, to fight any *mortal thing* they could produce against me. That night he retired late and staggering drunk to his garret, after having chained me up, sore and hungry, to my bedless barrel.

CHAPTER XVI.

TIGER ESCAPES FROM THE RAG-MAN AND REACHES HOME IN SAFETY.

As I lay awake, thinking of the hardness of my lot and of the happy home and friends from whom I had been severed, I fancied my collar felt somewhat looser; I therefore tried to extricate myself, and with some difficulty at last succeeded. With what joy did I find myself once more free! I hastened to the street, but was very much puzzled, at first, which way to take, as I had not been accustomed to city traveling. But, however, after running a few steps this way and a little way that, I recognized the road I had traveled under the rag-cart, and away I started, perfectly satisfied that neither Tom, Dick nor Harry could either overtake me or persuade me to retrace my steps. The morning sun had not yet tinted the eastern horizon, so that I soon reached the high-road without molestation. As I hastened onward my spirits revived, and the nearer I approached my home the faster I tripped along. I had but one skirmish on the road, as I preferred putting up with a slight insult rather than delay my journey. The impudent scoundrel who assailed me was an insignificant cur, who pounced on me unawares. I merely gave him one shake, when he sang out as though he was being murdered. I had no intention of the kind, but merely to chastise him for his insolence. In fine, I reached home in safety, though somewhat disfigured, worn, and jaded. When I reached the back-door, the cook immediately echoed my name through the whole house, which was fairly empty to welcome me. I was asked a hundred questions, rather in a reprimanding style; but they were so glad to see me back, that it all ended in my being extra-petted and extra-fed. My young master, being rather suspicious of my roving propensities, tied me up for a few days; but his fears were groundless, as I hadn't the most remote idea of exposing myself to any such casualities. Charley was delighted beyond measure, and visited me every hour in the day; and even the cat (with whom I had not been on the most intimate terms) came rubbing her back against me.

CHAPTER XVII.

TIGER'S WONDERFUL PATIENCE IN RAT-CATCHING.

In a short time, therefore, I was restored to my wonted freedom, and accompanied my master, as usual, in his youthful wanderings. One of his favorite amusements was ratting by the river-side. The banks were hollow with rats, and when he stamped they would bolt under water, upon which I was ready in an instant to dive after them, and generally succeeded in landing them lifeless at his feet. Sometimes they buried themselves in the mud, thus evading my grasp. I was so carried away by the sport, that I have often risen half-stifled to the surface without accomplishing my errand; though I generally seized them on my first spring, and have often dived into the mud with my game in my mouth, finding some little difficulty in extricating myself; but I was never discouraged at anything, and felt as though I never *should* relinquish my hold without particular orders.

The greatest feat I ever performed in rat-catching, demonstrating my patient resolution and determination, was in the catching of an old dog-rat who had taken up his headquarters in the beer-cellar. Upon the least alarm, he invariably and hastily retired through a hole in one of the paving-stones. Finding him far too cunning for me, I resolved patiently to watch for him, and devoted all my leisure hours to the task, sometimes gazing at the hole for eight or ten hours a day. I followed him up for months, till at last (I presume in one of his unguarded moments) I gripped him as he was making his exit from his subterraneous retreat, dealing him instant death. I shall never forget how proudly I marched around with him, and was unwilling to release him even for a moment. Nor was I satisfied with the approbation of my own immediate friends, but exhibited him at the abodes of several of our neighbors, after which I carefully buried him in a flower-border in front of the house. I cannot exactly scan my motives in this proceeding, but surely it was not from any notion of respect that I performed the last office to the object of my most deadly hate; on the contrary, I never visited his grave without evincing a disdainful contempt at his memory, and was often reprimanded for my ungentlemanly deportment among the tulips and hyacinths, as all knew full well that I was conscious of the trespass. I must avow it, I did transgress, almost against my will; but I felt so inwardly stung with hatred toward his detested race, that I felt an indignant joy in spurning his very resting-place.

CHAPTER XVIII.

TIGER'S HUNTING EXCURSIONS WITH GREYHOUND "FLEET."—HIS ABSENCE ACCOUNTED FOR.

I had been gradually forming an intimacy with Fleet, a fine young greyhound belonging to an acquaintance of my master's. We now and then met in our travels, but seldom did more than exchange the common civilities of the day: only on one or two occasions had we taken a short run together. So one afternoon, when I was rambling a short distance from the house, I noticed young Fleet cantering toward me, unaccompanied. We made our usual friendly salutes, when I observed something of a go-ahead expression in his eye, and clearly discovered that he was *in for a spree*, when he hastened to signify to me the very fact that he had left home with the express intention of peregrinating around the neighboring woods and fields. He used the most fascinating ejaculations and gestures to entice me to accompany him. After a little consideration, I consented to take a bit of a run with him. We were not long in deciding on our route. Off we *bolted* toward the woods, which we had scarcely entered when I got scent of a rabbit, and succeeded in hunting him out. Away we *put* full pelt after him, but he soon succeeded in concealing himself in some thick thorny underbrush. Fleet looked aghast, and kept running in all directions in search of the fugitive, presuming he had made his exit. But my nose was too sensitive to be deceived. I immediately ordered Fleet to keep on the alert, while I endeavored to dislodge our prey. I then forced my way into the thorny mass, dashing my way onward in spite of all obstacles, and soon succeeded in reaching his hiding-place. He sprang out instantaneously, like an arrow, but friend Fleet (who was as superior to me in sight as I was to him in scent) overtook and slew him ere I had scarcely emerged from the thicket. However, my presence was delayed only a few moments.

On my reaching Fleet, I perceived he had already commenced devouring our prize. This I stoutly resisted, sternly informing him that I was entitled to my share, and should insist on enforcing my claim. But as I did not feel inclined to be unnecessarily harsh, I allowed him to pull at one end while I tugged away at the other: thus we pretty equally divided it. After we had finished our repast and licked off our chops, Fleet immediately suggested the propriety of continuing the sport; but I firmly decided in the negative, as I was anxious to return home as quick as possible, in order to avoid any unpleasant feeling which might arise from my lengthened absence. As I exhibited marks of blood on my arrival, various hints were advanced as to the cause; but bearing no signs of violence on my person, I was acquitted of the charge of dog or cat-slaughter. It was therefore naturally concluded that I had only paid a visit to a neighboring slaughter-house, which I often frequented with my master for the purpose of obtaining a little refreshment.

A few days after, I again met with friend Fleet, when he proposed a second expedition in the same direction. This time I required but little persuasion, while he seemed far more delighted than before. We soon succeeded in the object of our excursion, and another fine fat rabbit was among the slain. But I arrived just in time to have the management of the booty myself, and dared Mr. Fleet to touch a hair of it; not from any selfish motive, but I had made up my mind to take it home uninjured to my master. I accordingly did so, to the great surprise and amusement of the whole family. I couldn't have stolen it—it was too fresh: I couldn't have caught it—I wasn't fast enough. How I got possession of it nobody knew. Thus we had our occasional hunts; and whenever I took a notion or did not happen to be hungry, I merely intimated my intention to Fleet, and he never dared to set a tooth on our prey after life was extinct. At last, from my constantly being missed, my master determined to watch me; and as Fleet and I were one day just in the heat of the chase, I heard my master's voice, while loud and angrily the woods echoed my name. Not till that moment had it occurred to me that I was acting wrong; but by the sound of his voice I was immediately reminded of many instances in which I had been called in, when only a few yards from the house, which made me feel truly guilty. I stopped short, relinquished the sport, and slunk ashamed up to my master, feeling that I deserved chastisement, though I seldom or ever knew him to be severe with me. He administered to me this time no other correction than a severe reprimand, which hurt my feelings far worse than a hundred blows. That was the last time Fleet and I ever met on such an errand. I saw him afterward occasionally, but having at once refused to re-admit him into my confidence, and rejecting the idea of resuming our accustomed companionship, he looked very coolly on me. In fact, he would scarcely treat me with common civility. Perhaps it was well for me that it was so, for he proved to be a wild, uneducated stripling, both reckless and headstrong, which proved his ruin. He had had some very severe lashings for killing chickens; was sorely punished for laming the turkey-gobbler; was almost killed for murdering his mistress' tortoise-shell cat; and not long after was shot dead while in the act of worrying a sheep. I had every reason to be thankful for a good education; though, with it all, I had my failings, which my natural perverseness would sometimes prompt me to encourage, against the better teachings of my knowledge and experience.

CHAPTER XIX.

TIGER, IN HIS MOST SERIOUS MOMENTS, CAN NEITHER FORGET NOR FORGIVE JOHNNY.

At the period of which I am now speaking I was full two years old; and although full of that buoyancy of spirits so common to our race, still the hey-day of pupdom had fled, and I began to settle down like a *reasonable* animal, seldom varying from my known duties, which I considered rather a pleasure than a task. Habit soon becomes second nature, and if our superiors would only bestow a little pains on our education, our gratitude and usefulness would amply repay them for the toil. We were intended as the helpers and protectors of man; and did he estimate us at only half our real worth, sheep-stealers and chicken-destroyers, curs and bone-grubbers, would be seldom heard of in our midst; his rest would not be disturbed by the yelping of a thousand ignorant mongrels, his friends would not be annoyed by their ill-timed liberties, nor his house tainted by their abominations: he might sleep secure, and enjoy that listless repose which we know so well how to ensure to him. They say we never sleep. Yes, we do; but with our ears as easily affected by sound, as the aspen-leaf by the zephyr. Our hearing is susceptible of the finest discernment: we are not often deceived by the innumerable murmurs of the ever-varying breeze, nor are our nerves agitated by the creaking door, the ricketty shutter, or the medley tones of insect and reptile. We can distinguish the footstep of a stranger, are ever faithful to our benefactors, and rare indeed has a traitor been found in our camp. In an uneducated state, I would ask, how far is man our superior? And even in his highest state of refinement, how necessary are we to complete his happiness! In how many points do we surpass him in discernment! Yea, how often do we supply him with knowledge, which his own *instinct* could never have dictated!

But as I go through my daily routine of duties, pastimes, and enjoyments, revenge! revenge! is brooding in my bosom. That confounded monkey haunts me day and night: every time I welcome my poor old Tripey, I scent the traces of his detested form. My blood, unbidden, curdles in my veins, and I feel as though a hundred fleas were dancing a hornpipe on my backbone. I sniff around her tattered robes, thinking perchance he may be cuddling there. I even ventured once to growl at the odor of his impested pelt, when the old Dame corrected me in unmeasured terms; and although I invariably paid all deference to her commands, I never succeeded in ridding myself of that strong-grounded antipathy with which I had been so deeply impregnated in my puphood. Yes, Tripey continued to visit me, and I was sometimes allowed to go home with her for an hour or two, when Truffle and Tom never failed to greet me with a hearty welcome. Every neighbor seemed pleased to see me, and contrasted my shining coat and plump proportions with my former poverty-stricken appearance and shapeless form. Truffle was really a worthy fellow, and was ever lavish in his expressions of joy when we met. He differed but little with me in regard to Johnny, but not being naturally gifted with the courage with which I was endowed, and being under constant surveillance, he had learned coolly to brook his insults, and generally to avoid coming in contact with him, except on particular occasions, when his services were required to satisfy the thirsty longings of his worthy mistress. As to Sam, I had never once forgotten his selling me to the rag-man, and ever afterwards I avoided his hypocritical caresses, and viewed him with mistrust. He would *sometimes* offer me an insignificant portion of his dumpling, but my feelings were set against him, and I almost felt inclined to growl at his feigned caresses. On one of these friendly visits to my old instructress, master Johnny undertook to assail me with the top of an old china tea-pot, giving me a rather severe blow on the head, which made me so far forget myself that I immediately flew at him and seized him by the neck, and was aggravated enough to have finished him there right; when I was checked by the screeching voice of old Tripey, accompanied by a smart leathern application to my ribs. Of course, I suddenly yielded to her authority, delighted as I felt at the agonizing screams of the detested Johnny.

CHAPTER XX.

TIGER CATCHES A THIEF, AND PROVES HIMSELF A TRUST-WORTHY GUARD.

One night, when, as usual, I was on guard taking my regular rounds, I heard a sudden and strange creaking of one of the cellar-windows. I hastened to the spot, when the only article visible to my comprehension, was a pair of pantaloons with boots at the end of them, worming their compressed carnalities through the iron bars. I immediately seized the most prominent part of their contents and held fast, planting my teeth deep into their owner, whose cries speedily aroused the inmates of the house. My young master was the first to arrive, when he exclaimed, "Seize him, Tiger! shake him, Tiger! good dog, Tiger!" upon which I redoubled my efforts, wofully lacerating the bleeding seat and understandings of the invader, who, on hearing my master's voice, pleaded so hard for mercy that I was called off; upon which he was dragged out and safely conveyed to the kitchen. After he was delivered up I ceased all idea of molesting him, as I considered I had accomplished all that could be required of me. I was praised beyond all measure for this determined and vigorous attack, and no price could have tempted my master to dispose of me; but I felt that I had done no more than my duty, and, in fact, at first I had felt some hesitation in pushing my authority to such an alarming extent. Nevertheless, seeing that I was so much praised as the principal actor in this rather comic tragedy, I felt increased confidence in myself; and to see me keeping the long and lonely watches of the night, you would naturally have supposed me to be "monarch of all I surveyed." Indeed, I thought more of the property which I held in trust, than I did either of myself or my little personals, and made it a rule to allow no one to convey anything off the premises without the presence of one of the household. On such occasions I seldom used any severe measures, especially with people occasionally employed on the premises, but simply notified to them by a gentle pinch, that I could not allow of the removal of any article without the presence of its owner.

On more than one occasion I was compelled to be somewhat violent—once, owing to the determination of a newly-hired laborer to make off with the wheelbarrow, which I certainly had no authority to permit. I merely took him gently by the ancle to advise him of the trespass; but as he seemed to disregard my warning, I increased the pressure; upon which he suddenly dropped the handles, and backed very cautiously toward the house, as I had then immediately released him. I followed close upon him, without meditating any farther interruption, but I never saw a poor fellow as frightened as he was. He kept shouting the whole way, sometimes to me, and sometimes to everybody, till he backed into the kitchen door. When he told his awful tale, it only excited laughter, and I was praised for my sagacity and intelligence; after which I allowed him to proceed, being satisfied that my young master must be aware of his movements, as he stood by when he resumed his work.

On another occasion I was near getting myself and my master into a very serious scrape. A loaferish-looking fellow had been in the habit of teazing me through the iron railings, and was near breaking my leg with a stone. I had often raved to get at him, as he poked me with a stick or pointed at me with his finger. One day, after he had worried me to the best of his ability, I noticed that the gate was on the jar. I forced my way out and grabbed him by the leg, hanging on to him till I had punished him severely. My master chanced to hear his cries and hastened to ascertain the cause, and was absolutely on the eve of dealing me a heavy blow, when the gardener remonstrated, assuring him that my annoyer had heartily deserved the punishment, as he had often witnessed his unprovoked attacks on me. But my good master, in consideration of his poverty, paid the doctor's bill and five weeks' wages, which he had forfeited from being unable to work. Long, long after this did he pass that way, but he never more molested me, nor did I even dream of contesting his passage.

CHAPTER XXI.

TIGER ACCOMPANIES HIS MASTER, WITH "PONTO" AND "MANSO," ON HIS SHOOTING EXCURSIONS.

I often went out with my master on his shooting excursions, accompanied by his father's favorite black pointer, Ponto, and his old setter, Manso. It was but seldom except on such occasions that we met together, as they were kenneled in a distant yard at the back of the stable, never being allowed the range of the garden and grounds. On these shooting trips my place was always in the rear, and I was seldom appealed to, except to search for dead or wounded game, which I invariably brought uninjured to my master's keeping. Ponto and Manso were well-trained, obedient animals. It really gave me great pleasure to witness their movements, and to see how steadily they kept to their work: they evidently understood motions with which I was totally unacquainted; moreover, their extraordinary patience puzzled me almost to death—old Manso especially. I have seen him stand for half an hour at a time over a hare, with Ponto behind, just as though they were pegged down. I knew that I dared not interfere, but I often thought it strange indeed, after all their pretended eagerness to come in contact with the object of their pursuit, to see them stand there like two monuments, and with apparent reluctance consent to *flush* their game. But they gave me plenty of work to catch wounded birds; and many a time, with disfigured countenance and besmeared person, have I succeeded in delivering to the anxious sportsmen what to *them* was irrecoverably lost; and although I was of too impatient a temperament to stand steadily longing for what was within my grasp, yet I was often of essential service, in starting to the sportman's view sundry winged bipeds and hairy quadrupeds, which were too safely ensconced to admit of *their* approaches. Besides, I was by far the best water-dog, and could swim and dive like a duck. Although Ponto and Manso were never backward in braving the watery element, I was the main dependence of my master in all these aquatic feats, as neither of them could boast of my energy and daring. While they were puddling and surveying, I was close on the trail of the fugitive, or following him beneath the bubbling surface of his native element. On many occasions neither Ponto nor Manto were considered necessary: as for hares, rabbits, and ducks, I was even considered their superior, and so habituated was I to my master's voice, that he could direct me in any way he pleased. Indeed, we understood each other's movements so well, that I required but little dictation. Although I was invariably inclined for an immediate advance on the enemy, I was too conscious of the superior judgment of my benefactor, to persist in any movement contrary to his commands. I could see clearly, though, that in many instances he depended on me alone, and waited as anxious on me for a decisive step, as I looked to him for my choice morsels. I was never so happy as when in his company, and we mutually enjoyed the fun, as away we dashed merrily along, freshening at every object of sport, and reposing only on an empty powder-flask or an exhausted shot-pouch. We indeed became so wedded to each other's society, that the shadow of the one indicated the presence of the other. His footsteps, however light, his voice, however indistinct to others, were as well known to me as my own bark. Not only could I divine where he was, but where he was not. I knew well the room where he slept; and when his window was first opened in the morning, we were the first of the family to exchange the compliments of the day. When he sallied forth without me, how sad I felt! how lonely the hours rolled away! Every distant sound awakened my attention, and every bell brought me to the gate. Such has been my anxiety in his absence, that, contrary to my known duty, I have deserted the house and started in search of him, many of his haunts being as well known to me as to himself. For this he would sometimes gently reprimand me, but soft indeed were his threats, and affectionate his warnings, well knowing that he alone was the cause of my disinterested transgression.

CHAPTER XXII.

TIGER SAVES THE LIFE OF HIS MASTER.

One night (well do I remember) my master had gone on horseback to spend the day with a friend at a distance. We both passed the day there very agreeably, though I confess I was somewhat tired, having traveled ten miles at my utmost speed. The weather was intensely cold. After having enjoyed a bountiful repast, as usual on such occasions, I lounged away the greater part of the day on the hearth-rug before the blazing fire. Night came on. It was late when my master's horse was ordered, and as he was a spirited animal, requiring neither whip nor spur, his feet tripped lightly over the king's highway, so that I, with my best powers, could barely keep pace with the rampant steed. But while I was pressing closely on him, he took a sudden fright, throwing my master into a deep quarry, and escaping at full and frantic speed toward home. Not so with me. I instantaneously descended to my master, whom I found still and speechless. I tried to arouse him, but in vain. I pulled his coat and licked his face, but he showed no signs of motion. I then became exceedingly alarmed, and concluded (after having remainded some time by his side, awaiting signals of animation) to hasten homeward and give information of my distress to the inmates of the house, and persuade them, if possible, to come to his relief. With this decision I started at full gallop, considering the most ingenious method of conveying the tidings of this sad catastrophe. My master was the only person who was thoroughly acquainted with my peculiar language and mode of expression, so that I naturally anticipated some difficulty in making myself understood. On reaching home, however, I hastened to scratch at the kitchen-door, which was soon opened to me: but, instead of awaiting my errand, the servant abruptly closed it on me and ordered me off. How reluctantly did I comply with the command! I paced up and down, considering what I should do, my anxiety increasing every step. Notwithstanding, I decided on making another attempt, in doing which I was abruptly assailed with a whip, grievously threatened, and imperiously ordered to bed. Imagine my feelings at the very introduction of my woful tale! I wandered to an fro, distracted and hopeless, and was on the eve of hastening back in despair to my master, when I thought I would yet make one desperate effort. I went to the front parlor window, and there exerted my lungs to their utmost extent, uttering the most incoherent, pitiful sounds, which succeeded at last in attracting the attention of the inmates. On hearing me, the first question was, "What dog is that?" and the question was echoed by the whole family: well it might be, for I scarcely knew myself what I was saying, so thoroughly agitated did I feel. The bell was rung, and the servant ordered to inquire what noisy brute was uttering such pitiful moanings. The night was bleak and frigid, and the bright, twinkling stars spoke volumes of frost and cold: but I felt it not; my thoughts centered alone on my absent friend. Such was my attachment, that I could have frozen to death by his side without a murmur. But I was bent on his deliverance.

O, how I longed for the power of speech! but as I was denied a speaking knowledge of the language of *man*, my only resort was to teach him my own; and I have been more than aggravated to think that our superiors should not even comprehend our most simple and ordinary methods of speech, while we are regaled with kicks, blows, huffs, and cuffs, if we do not instantaneously digest what we have never even had an opportunity of learning. In ordinary things we are not slow of comprehension; but if we are punished for unconscious faults, how are we to define when we really deserve correction? It is true, most of us require restraint, and many stubborn ones are reproved by timely chastisement; but ill-timed punishment and human ill-treatment often defeat their objects; rendering us abject cowards, degrading us to the level of outcast bone-grubbers, and incapacitating us from taking a stand in any respectable canine society.

But half a kitchen-full immediately bounced out, armed and unarmed, to encounter the noisy brute who had dared to disturb the sanctity of the cozy evening chat; when, to their great surprise, Tiger alone was there! It was with trembling joy that I welcomed their footsteps, almost dreading the total rejection of my suit. But he who had twice cast me from the door in anger, now bethought himself that something *might* be wrong. Seeing that I was not repulsed, I pushed my pleadings still further and ventured into the kitchen, determined to be understood by somebody. I ran out to the gate and back, as I thought all had made up their minds to ignore my errand: I even ventured to make a gentle attack on the footman's breeches. This convinced him that *something* must be *wrong*, especially as it occurred to him at the moment that I left home with my master in the morning, and had been absent all day. The information was conveyed to the parlor, and inquiries were immediately set on foot concerning what had become of my young master. Upon this the stableman entered, hastily announcing that the horse without a rider was standing at the gate. The mystery was at once solved, and Tiger was supposed to know all about it. I was instantaneously appealed to, and joyfully did I respond to their invitations. I signified to them to follow me. The stableman and footman were detailed for the journey. With their two lanterns they shivered after me, while I kept hurrying on out of their sight, continually returning to bid them hasten their steps, while (as I thought) my master might be sleeping in the arms of death.

On arriving at the spot where my master lay, I descend

ed the pit, while they followed me with the utmost caution and difficulty. They tried in vain to arouse him to consciousness: his pulse had apparently ceased to beat, his limbs were stiffened with cold. Sadly they bore him to his home, where shrieks of lamentation announced our arrival. I saw him stretched on the hearth-rug before a blazing fire, where all hands were employed in rubbing his frigid form and endeavoring to administer stimulating cordials. What was our mutual joy as we witnessed returning signs of animation! Yes, my master was again restored to me. His bruises happened to be light, but the frost had paralyzed his frame, and he must have *perished* but for Tiger—faithful, disinterested, affectionate Tiger! I expected no reward for his recovery, and was repaid a hundred-fold by the first kind word that escaped his lips.

But although I had done no more than I was prompted to by duty and affection, still all my acquaintances, on hearing of my devoted sagacity, lavished on me both gifts and praises, far more than I either merited or desired.

CHAPTER XXIII.

TIGER'S ACQUAINTANCE WITH THE NEWFOUNDLAND DOG ROSWELL.—HYDROPHOBIA.—TIGER'S COGITATIONS.

As I journeyed onward, my acquaintances multiplied; both biped and quadruped generally treating me with kindness and respect. Roswell, one of the finest specimens of the Newfoundland breed, was gradually extending himself into doghood. Although his harum-scarum ideas did not admit of his being allowed to range in my sphere, yet we saw each other almost daily; he was even allowed to accompany me in short trips with my young master. He was a dear, loving fellow, but was so lavish in his embraces that I sometimes had to threaten him for his puppish antics. Although I admit I really often enjoyed a good romp with this mammoth specimen of mirth and good humor, I felt disinclined to second him in all his puerile and boisterous ebullitions; consequently, when he importuned me with his unseemly frolics, I was compelled to enforce my authority; after which he seldom persisted in the annoyance. But he grew older and wiser, and waxed in knowledge as he waxed in stature. He had his training to go through, and although his tutor (the coachman) was not as apt as old Tripey, to whom I was so deeply indebted for all my primary lessons, still Roswell was naturally very intelligent, and in fetching and carrying he appeared more like a teacher than a scholar. Above all things, the old lady was sent for to teach him to carry *me;* moreover, to teach *me* to be carried by him; for I believe no one else would have persuaded me to consent to such an extraordinary method of traveling. However, with me her word was a law, and her authority I dared not dispute. She soon reconciled us both to the operation—*me* to get into a large hand-basket, and Roswell to carry me about. It became, at last, quite an amusement to us both, and I generally hastened to meet him, as I saw him coming with his basket in search of me. We often delighted the company together, and Roswell was ever the first to cry out, Enough! He was exceedingly well-behaved to me at all times, and I never knew him to take advantage of his superior strength; although I occasionally gave him sufficient cause for resentment, as I sometimes felt indisposed and absolutely refused to enter the traveling basket when he knowingly presented it to me. He was very fond of the water, but in spite of his enormous bulk, I invariably beat him in the race, when he bore his defeat with perfect good humor, and would even give way to me, rather than incur my displeasure. Poor fellow! he had scarcely reached his second year when he fell a victim to his passions. The object of his suit having disdainfully rejected his proposals, he became inconsolable, refusing all nourishment, and evincing a certain wildness of expression, a restless, irritable deportment, that even *I* dared not to approach him. Shortly after, he lost all possession of himself, became infuriated, and hastily fled from his home, unconscious and reckless of his course, mangling every living thing that crossed his path in a journey of twelve or fourteen miles; at the end of which a bullet traversed his heart, and Roswell fell on the bank of the river Severn, the victim of hydrophobia—the remains of a mad dog!

Several of my canine acquaintances have met with a similar fate, generally through the ignorance or neglect of their masters. Some were fed on unwholesome food, others lacked fresh water or were exposed to the rays of a burning sun, or, perhaps, like my worthy friend Roswell, were the victims of disappointed affection. But we are the by-word of all creation; and although many of our genus are over-petted and pampered, yet thousands, unconscious of our capacities and regardless of our welfare, entail misery on our race, by denying us the privilege of developing our almost reasoning instinct, thereby causing us to be condemned as skulking bone-grubbers and midnight marauders. Even the meanest of our kindred is faithful to his duty, and we need but kindness and good treatment, to induce us to perform cheerfully and readily, to our utmost capacity, all that we have been able to absorb from the teachings of man. I myself have suffered a hundred times from the indiscriminating ferocity and untutored impudence of my own class. Although I feared nothing but to disobey my master, could I submit to be imposed on and insulted by every overgrown specimen of perverted dogdom? True, I have many a time indignantly retired, rather than converse or even exchange civilities with such ill-bred, untutored quadrupeds; yet, on various occasions, my business was such as to demand my presence amid a motley assemblage of rampant ignorance and insolence. At such meetings I have found myself compelled to resist and repel all unprovoked attacks, and have generally succeeded in ridding myself of the aggressors. Indeed, I have been pounced upon by a whole party of these lawless rowdies, and have come out both lacerated and defaced. These attacks had engendered in me a certain mistrust of the whole fraternity, so that with all strangers I assumed a dignified, distant, self-confident demeanor, which seldom failed to impose respect even from the most refractory. But a word from my master was enough: cat, dog, badger, bull, or bear, all were one to me. At his command I seized my antagonist, regardless of danger, thoughtless of my own safety, and bent on destruction. He, and he alone, could restrain my fury, and even *then* did I reluctantly obey his commands, such was the violence of my excited temper. I was born so, and to conquer it has been the main study of my life, though I succeeded only to a certain extent; but without education I might have lived a perfect hyena, lacerating friend and foe, seeking for blood, a scourge to the flock and the pest of society.

CHAPTER XXIV.

TIGER RAT-KILLING WITH A HOST OF HIS ASSOCIATES.—GREAT EXCITEMENT IN THE WHEAT-STACK.

But my own immediate neighborhood was far from being deficient in useful and trustworthy members of human and canine society. The farmers were plundered and annoyed to an alarming extent by swarms of rats, who held, for a season, undisputed possession of their wheat-stacks. When such was known to be the case, a general killing-day was announced, and we, who delighted in the destruction of these detestable vermin, held a general meeting for the purpose of concerting measures for signing their death-warrants. Sometimes twenty or thirty of us would post ourselves in military order around an immense wheat-rick, and as sheaf by sheaf was thrown into the wagon, we anxiously awaited an opportunity of distinguishing ourselves by ridding society of these unwelcome intruders. Seldom did any escape our grasp, when Brandy, Pinch, Snap, Vick, and Rip; Bill, Jack, and Cribb; Fan, Bob, and Trip, together with my *respectful self*, were found on guard.

To the lovers of fun this must have been a real treat, to see how each, backed by his master, waited with bursting gaze to pounce on every fugitive as he ventured on flight. Sometimes a troop would venture out at once: then for the hallooing, the hustling and squeaking, the shaking and pounding! The game was truly alive, and the names of Tiger, Cribb, Jack, Snap, and the rest of our fraternity, were continually sounded with ecstatic joy, as their struggling victims uttered their farewell squeaks. Old Tripey seldom failed to be present on these important occasions, when her shrill voice was heard above all cheers and laughter, boasting of her Tiger, and offering to stake a whole basket of tripe that I would beat them all. Friend Truffle never ventured within twenty yards of the scene of action, but was generally heard raising his yelp in timid exultation; yet on the approach of a rat, he preferred making room for one of his bolder brethren, rather than expose his countenance to be disfigured. The fact is, when he was quite young, Tripey was so proud of him and so conscious of his abilities, that she ventured to bring him into close contact with a high-fed, fully-developed dog-rat. Friend Truffle made a bold and desperate attack on him, when the despairing beast traversed his upper jaw with his pointed grinders, causing poor young Truffle to utter the most piercing yells, as he vainly endeavored to disengage his bleeding muzzle from the death-like gripe of his pugnacious foe, who, however, effected his escape without being seriously wounded. This was master Truffle's first lesson, and it so impregnated him with the idea of the omnipotence of rats on youthful countenances, that Tripey herself, with her powers of almost canine persuasion, could never demonstrate to him the necessity of a second encounter. His decision of character in this instance was admirable. He had made up his mind, no doubt after mature consideration, not to expose himself to such casualties for the future. Thus, he generally stood aloof on these perilous rendezvous. I really think he was somewhat amused with the sport, although he invariably kept at such a respectful distance.

On reaching near the bottom of the stack the excitement increased, many of the invaders being determined to remain as long as there was the least hope of shelter. But as the sheaves thinned off they swarmed out in droves, the whole company of us dashing right and left, fore and aft, north, south, east, and west, and a general melee ensued, causing wholesale slaughter among these houseless interlopers, few of whom ever escaped to cross the frontier. After the wind-up, the carcasses of the slain were numbered, and a sight it was, to see our separate piles of exterminated vermin, as we each stood by, silently glorying over their blood-stained carcasses, our numerous tails wagging silently in concert. How joyfully we viewed our lifeless prey! regretting only that we could not recall them to life, to enjoy once more their final squeak. As each competitor had to pay sixpence or a shilling to the owner of the dog who killed the most rats, I was invariably awarded the premiums, which were as regularly handed over to poor old Tripey, who caused the valley to ring with my praises, and furnished herself many a gratuitous night's lodging in the ditch, generally not far distant from her last tippling-house.

CHAPTER XXV.

JOHNNY PICKS THE MAGPIE, SPOILS THE TRIPE, AND IS SOLD TO AN ORGAN GRINDER.

Great was my surprise, as I paid my usual visit to the old dame, on observing the absence of one of our old boarders. That confounded Johnny was no longer at his post; but as Tripey kept repeating his name to me, I expected every moment to see him make his appearance. But no—Johnny was clean gone. He was now the property of an Italian organ-grinder, who had purchased him of the old lady, in the presence of an empty tripe-basket and a husky throat. I doubt whether the empty tripe-basket and husky throat alone would have tempted my old mistress to dispose of him; but she had been so enraged by his malicious antics, the day before, that she vowed and protested, aye, absolutely *swore*, he should nevèr stop another night in her house. In her absence the villain had broken loose, and after having mixed up the boiling tripe with soot and ashes, had taken down her favorite magpie, picked every feather off his tortured pelt, and on her arrival, was in the act of amusing himself in assisting him to hobble about in shapeless nudity.

Tripey was well-nigh frantic with rage, and so belabored his trembling hide that his screams attracted the neighbors, who with difficulty succeeded in respiting his life. All that night she was heard to utter little more than three words—"*monkey! tripe!* and *magpie!*" while Sam, who giggled out indignant bursts of the most decided delight at the occurrence, was occasionally saluted with a tea-kettle, frying-pan, or three-legged stool, accompanied by the most solemn vows to deprive him *for ever* of his favorite pot-skimmings. Truffle appeared much gayer than usual, delighted with Johnny's absence; testifying his satisfaction by running backward and forward to his late dormitory, and inviting me to join him in his exultations. But the poor blackbird had not yet recovered his fright, for he had trembled lest he should share the fate of his unlucky comrade, and it was long ere he resumed his wonted loquacity.

CHAPTER XXVI.

TIGER IS AVENGED, AND SLAYS THE DETESTED JOHNNY.

But that vile scoundrel Johnny's days were numbered. As I happened one day to be taking an airing with my master, who was on horseback, I was suddenly startled by the sound of an organ proceeding from a side-road. I chanced to cast a glance that way, as my master was slowly pacing onward, when I perceived the hated Johnny dancing to the music. I hesitated for a moment as to the propriety of diverging from my path, bethinking me of the thousand insults he had heaped upon me, his oft-repeated tugs, pulls, and pinches, his sneaking, vicious grins, his treachery and hypocrisy. I stood doubting between my duty and my ruling passion, when I suddenly decided on the most desperate revenge. Making a few hasty bounds, I seized my adversary by the throat, and, reckless of his agonizing shrieks and of the blows inflicted on me by the astonished spectators, I continued to deepen my impressions on him, as he vainly implored for mercy. My passions were so completely aroused, that I believe that even death itself would have found my teeth buried in his hated form. But I was in the act of giving him his final shake, when my master, attracted by the medley uproar, and I not answering to his call, hastily galloped to the scene of action, dismounted, and insisted on my relaxing my hold. Never did I so unwillingly obey his commands, for although considerably pounded and somewhat disfigured in my physiognomy, I felt myself more than a match for a hundred monkeys. But the die was cast. On releasing my hold, Johnny opened his eyes, stretched his legs, curled his tail, and breathed his last in my presence; and I, revengeful Tiger, would have forfeited the best pot of tripe that my old mistress had ever cooked, for the privilege even of a single shake at my lifeless oppressor. The crowd had now decided on finishing me; but as my master grasped me in his arms to save me from their attacks, they withdrew to condole with the almost disconsolate and monkeyless organ-grinder. My master, however, previous to our leaving, compensated him for his loss, with the reasonable advice to keep his monkeys at home. It was not till after he settled the bill, that he recognized the remains of the well-known Johnny; and as he had long been aware of my deserved hatred toward him for his numerous unprovoked annoyances, I believe he almost pardoned me for ridding myself of an enemy, who for years had succeeded in escaping my resentment: besides, he had ever such an exalted opinion of me, that I believe he thought me scarcely capable of doing wrong. Although I confess I was occasionally tempted to commit some acts of insubordination, still, as he considered me so far superior in talents and education to the majority of our race, to say nothing of my having preserved his property and saved his life, he seldom spoke to me in anger or threatened me with stripes.

CHAPTER XXVII.

TIGER'S FRIEND, "TRUSTY," THE SHEPHERD-DOG.

But we often, in our sporting trips, spent half the day in indulging among the farmers, where we enjoyed good fare and a hearty welcome. The gun reposed in the chimney corner, my master in the beehive chair, while I lay stretched to my utmost length or condensed to my shortest growth, fronting the blazing faggot or smouldering log, except at intervals, when I fancied a stroll in the surrounding fields.

At one of these rustic depots of fat bacon and good humor, I had become intimately acquainted with my worthy friend Trusty, a shepherd-dog of excellent breeding and of somewhat refined education. Although he could neither boast of town tricks nor city antics, he was quite an adept in his profession, and occasionally put me to the blush by his wonderful performances. In spite of his partiality for me, and notwithstanding my oft-repeated invitations, he never would consent even to a ramble or a romp, till his sheep were safely folded or his presence dispensed with. No sheep so wandering, but he could restore it to the flock; none so rampant, but he could hold him in safety; not one so restive, but must obey his commands. He would take them out and guide them home: the sound of his voice alone sufficed to warn the most inexperienced, to check the most unruly. Though none appeared to fear, yet all felt bound to obey him. The tender lamb, with instinctive consciousness of safety, reposed peacefully by his side, and the whole flock submitted to his gentle yet decisive commands. He watched them by day and guarded them by night, and the faithful Trusty was never known to neglect his duty or desert his flock. His temper was often put to the test by the obstreperous subjects of his charge, but so gentle were his corrections that none bore marks of his resentment. For my part, I have always considered myself of too irritable a disposition to undertake the management of such a diversity of tempers, often wondering how so gentle a sway should command universal respect. His equanimity of temper was really astonishing, and certainly well befitting his station and responsibilities. In private life he was none the less amiable. By his gentle manners, his familiar yet unobtrusive deportment, he had secured the admiration and respect of a large circle of acquaintances. Often, in his leisure intervals, have we roved the fields together, cooled ourselves in the fish-pond, and polished ourselves in the grass; and not even in our most boisterous diversions have I known a single hasty or unkind expression to mar our friendly perambulations. What a strange contrast between my learned friend Trusty, and the countless host of noisy mongrels, who, disturbed by every changing breeze, and priding themselves in their unmeaning and ceaseless yelping, charmed with the echo of their own insignificance, live unenvied and unlamented! Education might have moulded them to be both useful and profitable members of society; but, alas! they were either considered unworthy, or their owners were careless of the task.

CHAPTER XXVIII.

TIGER'S ATTACHMENT TO "VICK," A FEMALE BLACK-AND-TAN TERRIER.—HER PROPERTIES AND CHARACTERISTICS.

My acquaintances were not *all* of the masculine gender; I had many deserving favorites among the opposite sex; and I flatter myself, that although I was perhaps too prone to be somewhat haughty and vindictive toward many of my brethren, not in the whole course of my canine career can I recall a single instance of the slightest rudeness or inattention, much less of hostility, even to the most unrefined of females. This feeling was the inborn production of my own native instinct: not a word on the subject had even been whispered to me in my early days, nor hinted as I ripened in education and experience. In this point, *even we* of inferior mould may be said to surpass untutored manhood—aye, even civilized monsters of humanity, refined bipeds of the highest grade; many of whom neglect, abuse, and even torture those delicate forms, which their superior reason has bid them to respect and cherish. But far be it from me to establish my own reputation, by heaping infamy on those whose mandates I was born to obey. Still, I shall be proud indeed if, by extolling our virtues and exposing our failings, I should succeed in presenting such a true and living picture of ourselves as may engage those who feel somewhat interested in our behalf, to study our nature, inclinations, and habits, to cultivate our flexible, quadrupedal intellects, thus giving us a fair opportunity of demonstrating that we were not born to howl and growl, to annoy and destroy, but to be the friends and guardians, the helpers and companions of man; ever disinterested and faithful in his service, ready and willing to execute his commands.

But I can't help thinking of several of my female acquaintances. One in particular, Vick, an elegant, fine bred, black-and-tan terrier, who belonged to an old friend of my master. She was one of the prettiest creatures I ever saw; such a lovely form and such gentle manners, so affable and obliging—in fine, so thoroughly educated, that she rendered herself worthy of my highest estimation. We performed many extraordinary tricks together for the amusement of our friends, and I am not ashamed to confess that she often outwitted me, as she seemed intimate with the names of articles that I never even heard of. Out of a dozen, she could pick out any one named, and hand it to any person pointed out. She would even ransack the pockets of a whole party, in search of anything that was lost; would lead the young child about like a mother, and, when in the cradle, would watch over it as tenderly. She was as quick as lightning in the destruction of all kinds of vermin, took letters to the post-office, could ring the bell, open and shut the door, put out the candle, and as a proof of her nocturnal fidelity, she never absented herself from her master's door during his hours of slumber. These are only a *few* of her acquirements; but her amiable, winning disposition was, to me, far more endearing than all her educational performances; and I must avow I have occasionally felt rather jealous that she should be more noticed and petted than myself. Yes, I became devotedly attached to her, and more than once have I incurred my master's displeasure, for having absented myself from home to enjoy the pleasure of her society. I felt, on these occasions, a consciousness of neglecting my duty, but my impulses were too powerful for canine resistance—my education was unequal to their government, and my will too stubborn to be controlled, when Vicky was the object of my pursuit, the desire of my heart, the anchor of my hopes. But alas!

I was not without rivals. Many a duel have I fought, and received many a wound, in support of my jealous disposition and headstrong attachment. But Vicky was fickle, and complacently admitted the attentions of a variety of suitors. This was her greatest defect; and although I am far from declaring that she alone was mistress of my affections, yet I could not but feel irritated, and even enraged, with any interloper who dared to make her any advances in my presence. She was the innocent cause of leading me into some serious scrapes: I was, nevertheless, unremitting in my attentions, occasionally regardless even of the interests of him I was wont to respect.

CHAPTER XXIX.

TIGER BOUND FOR SPAIN.—HIS VISIT TO LONDON.

But "there is a tide in the affairs of" dogs as well as of men, and I for a season was to be severed from all my old acquaintances, both human and canine. My master was bound for a journey into Spain, and Tiger, the faithful Tiger, *must* be the companion of his travels. Little did I imagine the cause of the excitement, when the whole family crowded around us with their parting embraces. Even old Tripey, aware of our departure, stood whimpering with Truffle by her side, as we mounted the stage-coach which was to convey us on our way to London. She hugged and kissed me, bidding me (as she thought) a "long and last farewell." Truffle gave me a very significant wag, the old lady burst into tears, and away we went. Though it was not the first time I had rode in a carriage, this parting seemed somewhat strange to me. True, I felt no regret, heaved not a sigh, nor shed a single tear, but was as usual delighted beyond measure at the prospect before me—such as I had ever realized with my master—good treatment, good fare, and good sport. On arriving in the great city, I was almost petrified with astonishment, and could easily have persuaded myself that a shadow of fear had crossed my somewhat bewildered imagination. As I dodged my master among dense masses of boots and shoes, fearing I might be the peculiar subject of attraction, I had not the remotest idea of whither he was hurrying me, although, regardless of all obstacles, I kept worming my way onward, dreading lest I should not only lose myself, but my only friend and protector. During our short stay, I dared not absent myself a moment from his side; by his feet at the dining-table, by his heels in his meanderings, and in his sleeping-hours I neither desired nor was allowed to be out of his presence. Unaccustomed to city life, though never for a moment wishing to desert my master, I often longed for my cherished and happy home in the country, where my footsteps were free and my circuit undefined. But here, though pampered with all the delicacies of the season, and extolled by the flattery of a thousand strangers, I fattened and lolled at the expense of my spirits, leading a monotonous and uninteresting life: no Charley, or Vicky, or Pastor, or Truffle, to enliven my spirits! no ratting, no swimming, not a green field to ramble in, not a rabbit to hunt! After a few long weeks, in which I had revelled in gluttony, indolence, and inactivity, I found myself, in company with my master, on board ship, completely surrounded with water in the stormy Bay of Biscay. I first began scrutinizing every hole and corner in the vessel, to satisfy myself of my whereabouts and ascertain the length of my range. As I wandered from port-hole to port-hole, and viewed all around the expanse of rolling waters, I declined casting myself on their turbid bosom, fearing that I might not be able to return; so I coolly settled down with my master, determined to stick to the ship and patiently await his commands.

CHAPTER XXX.

TIGER'S FIRST LANDING IN SPAIN.

A few stormy days landed us on a foreign soil. But to me the country was far less strange than the people, as their queer, discordant notes were to me indeed incomprehensible. Although their conversation was often addressed to me, I gave but little heed to (I presumed) their introductory remarks, feeling rather inclined to shrink from notes of such doubtful import. But my master soon explained to me the meaning of a variety of terms, so that in a month or two I was thoroughly competent to execute many of his orders in Spanish as well as in English. Indeed, the natives considered me a very apt scholar, remarking that sundry bipeds of human extraction made far less progress than myself. Having previously acquired a partial understanding of the French language, I was no doubt the better prepared to absorb ideas in a kindred brogue. However, I gradually became naturalized to my new habits, and I must say I never met with more real kindness, even in my most domestic rovings. I soon began to form acquaintances of my own race, and, as a general rule, I confess they were far less quarrelsome and snarlish than the majority of English canines. Whether there was anything in my appearance calculated to command fear or respect, is not for me to decide, but I observed a certain shyness in their approaches toward me, and a general unwillingness among them even to exchange with me the common civilities of the day. I have often, on my approach, witnessed the dispersal of a whole company, who either lacked courage to face me, or doubted the propriety of venturing familiarities with strangers.

CHAPTER XXXI.

TIGER'S ACQUAINTANCE WITH "LINDA," A FEMALE SPANISH POINTER.

Notwithstanding this, I met with some very agreeable society, especially in Linda, a female pointer, who occasionally accompanied us in our sporting jaunts. She did not reside with us, but boarded at the house of a poor peasant, where she was endowed with a numerous offspring, two of which added to the pleasure of our homeward trip to England. There we often visited her and her motley scions. Old Tripey's cottage was a palace indeed, when *contrasted* with the unvarnished aspect of her keeper's dwelling. Four pebbled walls and a raftered roof, encased with mud, (enclosing the bare earth beneath,) formed the solitary apartment of a numerous family, comprising Linda's keeper, his wife, and three children, whose elevated and tattered couch indicated their noble descent and pedigree, and occupied the most important angle of this distinguished abode. In the opposite corner lay Linda and her progeny, contentedly cuddled away among a few leaves of Indian corn. In the third corner, within a small enclosure, grunted two thriving hogs, whose snouts I could seldom refrain from pinching, when they intruded themselves to my notice. The fourth was the nightly abode of the feathered tribe, whose stately and pugnacious senior was ever the first to announce approaching dawn, arousing the happy inmates of this peaceful dwelling. To complete the whole, under the dormitory of the human family burrowed a troop of rabbits, one of which I had inadvertently slaughtered, previous to my being initiated into the domestic arrangements of this blissful amalgamation of hair, bristles, fur, and feathers. A blazing fire in the centre, surrounded by the *lords* of creation, occasionally shed its glow to the remotest corner of this favored domicil, while the smoke crept lazily out of the glassless window and open door. But this varied group all fared alike, and the withdrawal of the *higher* *branches* of the family from the smoking emporium of Indian bread and *ferrapas*,* was a signal for the *inferiors* to prepare for action. I have been present on these occasions, but have invariably refused their proffered hospitality, as quite unsuited to the palate of the celebrated Tiger. But Linda was contented and happy—far from displaying in her person any lack of the necessaries or comforts of life, although she evinced an almost ecstatic delight at the very odor of a meal from my master's table, and was never known to take supper on her return home. We have had many delightful trips together, in company with my master. She attended to the quail and partridge department, while I busied myself in hunting up rabbits, squirrels, foxes, etc. We generally had plenty of sport, but I believe I could have killed a hundred rats while she stood gazing at a single partridge. As she understood no other language than her native Spanish, and I was often in her company, I improved rapidly in comprehending my master's orders, as they were delivered to her in that language. I was, above all, delighted to find that she understood our English canine lingo as well as I did myself: in fact, it was this that struck me on my first landing—that even the most common-looking mongrel was on the most intimate terms with all the different and difficult intonations of barking, howling, snarling, whining, yelling, growling, and a hundred other indicative notes, which no foreign race has scarcely ever taken the pains to interpret. No: unfortunately for us, we are ofttimes unable to convey our ideas to our superiors, in spite of our varied notes and expressive looks, and wonder why man should be so slow of comprehension, so inattentive to our wants, so careless of our welfare.

* The provincial term for boiled Indian meal.

CHAPTER XXXII.

TIGER INTRODUCES US TO HIS FRIEND "BLANCO," A SPANISH SETTER.

Blanco, too, was a worthy fellow, a white setter of superior stamp. We met almost daily in our evening promenades, and amused ourselves in company with our masters, dashing into the sea and frolicking together. Not an angry sound ever passed between Blanco and me, as we walked side by side, sometimes for hours, in happy communion. This faithful game-hunter never left his master without orders, neither could he be tempted to follow another; but at his command would accompany (though sometimes reluctantly) the greatest alien: neither would he allow any one to touch him without his master's consent; after which, he was delighted with the stranger's caresses. I admired him for this, as we both had undergone the same teachings, and we have occasionally changed masters for a season; I was then ordered to follow his master and he to accompany mine. At such times I suppose our feelings were somewhat similar, as we both seemed to consider it rather unkind. Although Blanco was occasionally the whole day off with us, *my* master was so afraid of anything happening to me, that he would never consent to my lengthened absence. Blanco had a wonderful memory: for if anything had been pointed out to him a mile off, in the morning, he would fetch it at any time of the day; would retrace an hour's march to find what was lost, allowed no one, without orders, to enter his master's bedroom, roused him up every morning at the accustomed hour, fetched his hat, cane, etc., and led the horse to water. Many other useful offices did Blanco perform, in perfect good humor, and was never so delighted as when serving his benefactor. Besides, he was a perfect hunter, carefully presenting every trophy uninjured to his master, and tiring only over a gameless country or a luckless fowling-piece. What useful animals we are! If man only had enough of us, well trained and educated, he might almost dispense with half of his hireling two-legged assistants, many of whom serve him only to serve themselves; while we, without fee or reward, scour the mountain, thread the meadow, and penetrate the forest, in search of his sustenance, contented with the crumbs that fall from his table, and even when starving by his side, remain faithful even unto death.

CHAPTER XXXIII.

TIGER JOINS THE WOLF-HUNT IN THE PYRENEES, IN COMPANY WITH "PASTOR," "LÉON," ETC.

But I had a task to perform for which I considered myself wholly incompetent, though I *did* prove of essential service. There was to be a wolf-hunt! I did not consider myself a match for a wolf, in spite of my master having declared *he* was not afraid to venture me. Accordingly, we started for a Pyreneean wolf-hunt. Such an assemblage of peasants I never saw. They came by hundreds, well armed with shovel, pickaxe, spade, hoe, pistol, blunderbuss, gun, sword, club, and spade—in fine, every instrument they could lay their hands on. I was somewhat startled at the sight of such a ferocious set of bipeds, and rather excited lest they might intend me some greivous bodily harm; but they all seemed delighted to make my acquaintance, as they all surrounded me and examined me from tip to toe, declaring they had never seen anything like *me* before. But when my master told them that I was going to stir the wolf out of the almost impenetrable furze and underwood, they smiled very doubtfully, looking at each other in vacant astonishment. They were accompanied by several noble, majestic canines, Pyreneean or Alpine shepherd-dogs, vastly superior to me in nerve and muscle, and well capable of entering into single combat with the most ferocious wolf; but, not only were they too bulky to thread themselves into his dense retreat, but it also struck me they were too careful of themselves to venture on the experiment. Still, they were noble and brave, and treated me with the greatest civility. They certainly seemed determined to carry home a correct account of my geometrical proportions, as they completely registered my person from stem to stern. As this operation was performed with perfect good humor, without any unpleasant or derogatory remarks on their part, I coolly submitted to their scrutinizing examination.

These preliminaries being concluded, the signal was given and the hunters formed a circle of perhaps a mile in diameter, which lessened as we drew nearer the centre, thus gradually approaching the field of battle. Now for the tug of war! The cry *Lobo!** *Lobo! Lobo!* was shouted and echoed by a hundred tongues. Away sped the wolf, dashing wildly along, Pastor and Leon pressing closely on his heels; but he soon buried himself in the matted furze, and bid them defiance. My turn was now come. I had joined in the chase, but they were fleeter than I. While they were baying furiously, pacing hither and thither around the cowardly fugitive, my master ordered me to force my way to his matted lair.. I bold and fearlessly bored my way through bush and bramble, thorn and briar, till I espied the glaring daylights of my desperate adversary. I had never found myself face to face with such a fearful antagonist; but I was *in for it*, and as I had never yet beat a retreat, such an inglorious resolve did not even threaten me now. Often had I encountered rat, cat, weasel and polecat, fox and badger; but this was game of a higher order, demanding heavier metal and more extensive ivories than I could boast. What I lacked, then, in dimensions, had to be atoned for in pluck. Fearless, reckless, and desperate, I threw myself wildly on him, first seizing him by the fore-leg, when I immediately felt his pointed grinders lacerating my shoulders; but I was too earnest and maddened to relax my hold, which punished him to that degree, that, speedily releasing me, he uttered a most frightful yell, thinking perchance to frighten me into terms; failing in which, he bolted from his seclusion, dragging me after

**Lobo*, wolf.

him, till, reaching the open space, he was seized by Pastor and Leon, who, *with my assistance*, dispatched him with a few simple embraces of their capacious jaws. My praises "rang the regions round," after several of these hazardous and bloody encounters, and many were the visits paid me from all quarters. Large amounts were continually offered for me, but my master had made up his mind that I should never be owned by another; that, as I afforded him so much amusement and satisfaction, had preserved his property and saved his life, I should still be his companion in prosperity and adversity.

CHAPTER XXXIV.

TIGER MEETS WITH HIS OLD FRIEND "SOTO."—HIS OPINION OF POODLES.

Of all the canine acquaintances I had formed in Spain, none had afforded me more pleasure than I experienced in meeting my old friend Soto, an elegant cocker-spaniel, which my master had previously sent from England as a present to his friend, the Marquis of V——. We had been on the most intimate terms in England, where, although rather wild and uneducated, he was of an inoffensive and playful disposition. In spite of his having never undergone any regular course of instruction, he had naturally absorbed a certain suavity of manners which rendered him a general favorite. More than a year had passed away previous to his leaving England, and Soto had not greeted us as we approached his old master's dwelling. True, I had often missed his merry scamper and sprightly dance, but in the multitude of my recreative and business occupations I had scarcely felt his absence. What was my surprise and joy when I was introduced to him, as he was reclining on a gilded couch, the admired of all, a pattern of canine elegance and refinement! On observing my presence, he immediately descended, somewhat abruptly, appearing to consider me as an intruder. I addressed him in intimate terms, but he still appeared (as I thought) somewhat loth to acknowledge me; but as I was in the act of indicating to him my willingness for one of our old-fashioned gallopades, he immediately recognized me, when, after our mutual congratulations, he showed me all over the premises, with evident signs of masterly satisfaction and delight. One thing astonished me beyond measure—to hear him listen to a long confab in Spanish with the most marked attention, appearing inwardly to digest every syllable, while I sat by, wondering what it all signified, as, with the exception of a chance word or two, I was utterly at a loss to comprehend such an impenetrable compound. But Soto evidently delighted in the conversation, and performed many singular and curious feats, which he never could have accomplished without being perfectly conversant with the nature of his commands. Like myself, he wiped his feet thoroughly clean, previous to entering the house, was a faithful guard to his master's bedroom, could sit up or stand up, and was perfect in several other of my favorite acts. Although I knew much more than he did, he had also acquired much that I had not. He invariably called up all the servants, was ready with his master's boots in the morning and his slippers at night, knew how to open and shut the door, would gently force the cat from parlor to kitchen, and from kitchen to parlor, and had never been known to quit the house *alone* on any pretense whatever. In fact, he was a genteel, well-informed, praiseworthy spaniel, far superior in person, manners, and education, to the majority of quadrupeds in that region. He understood but a few words of English; and notwithstanding his having recognized both my master and me shortly after our arrival, he seemed somewhat confounded at the very sound of the language of his native country. We are none of us fond of foreign languages, and are seldom known to persist in an attack when reprimanded in a foreign tongue. In my own country, I have witnessed some of the most courageous of our race sneaking off abruptly from a meditated attack, on being imperiously saluted with a volley of foreign gibberish. I was delighted with my trip to Spain, but somewhat astonished at seeing so few of my own particular caste. In Madrid I was surrounded by a host of poodles on various occasions, but they merely expressed their satisfaction on forming my acquaintance; and, far from causing me any annoyance, I could scarcely repress my feelings of pride and superiority as I marched stiffly among them. If by chance they felt inclined to take any liberties with me, a single growl would scatter a whole company. But timid and pusillanimous as they were, there were many knowing ones among them, who excelled in dancing and many pleasing diversions. In fact, although they appeared to lead an idle and somewhat useless life, yet they seemed the necessary appendage to coquetry and fashion.

CHAPTER XXXV.

TIGER'S RETURN TO ENGLAND.—REVISITS HIS OLD CRONIES.

Our journey home was only a repetition of former scenes. Although I had experienced no regret in leaving my birthplace and friends while in my master's company, yet great indeed was my joy on finding myself once more in my accustomed haunts. Notwithstanding my having been absent only a few months, I experienced the most inexpressible pleasure in meeting my old friends, and was received by them all (I doubt not) with heartfelt congratulations. I really thought old Tripey would have squeezed me to death. Her tongue rattled away for an hour; she asked me a thousand questions, (I suppose,) which I should have liked very much to have answered in a more expressive manner than by a simple ebullition of canine whimperings, accompanied by a rapid agitation of the extremity; but as our interview terminated satisfactory to us both, why should I complain? If I could really speak, I might often get myself into trouble, as I might perchance upbraid many who had the power to oppress me. Poor Truffle (who was no hypocrite) was wonderfully elated on meeting me. Though he was now getting old, he scampered round me like a juvenile, and absolutely sprang over me for joy. When I paid him a visit he was much freer than usual, as there was no Johnny now to keep him in check. The blackbird was still there, and appeared to welcome me as I entered, stretching his neck out of his wicker cage while the old lady announced to him my arrival, to which he assented by quaintly enunciating "Tiger! Tiger!—Johnny! Johnny!" These last words recalled more forcibly to my recollection all my former adventures with the hated Johnny, particularly our last fatal encounter. But he had made such a deep impression on the tablets of my memory, that at the sound of his name, I felt the very hairs (as I thought) creeping off my back: his image stared me in the face. I immediately flew to his old corner, and continued hunting around in all directions. The old dame noticed me, and as she repeated his name, my anger was the more aroused. I hastily and madly searched every nook and corner, and with difficulty was I persuaded to relinquish the chase, as I firmly believed he must have been purposely hidden from my sight.

Many pleasurable meetings I had in revisiting all my old acquaintances, both of my master's intimates and my own: but I can't account for it—although I was ever pleased in my friendly intercourse with many of my own class, and delighted in joining their sports, I never could look on the most refined of them as my equals. I never followed them, I never obeyed them, I never asked any favors of them, and seldom yielded to their requests. Had the whole united fraternity elected me their chief, I should have indignantly spurned the honor, preferring a half-picked bone at my master's feet to the united adulations of concentrated dogdom.

CHAPTER XXXVI.

TIGER BIDS FAREWELL TO ALL HIS ENGLISH ACQUAINTANCES, AND EMIGRATES.—INCIDENTS OF HIS PASSAGE ACROSS THE ATLANTIC, ETC.

But little did I suspect that I was so soon to bid a long and final farewell to the associates of my youth and doghood, the companions of my sports and pastimes. Good-bye, cats, rats, polecats, foxes, rabbits, and weasels! Adieu, Charley, Manso, Roswell, Ponto, Vick and Trusty; Dick, Jack, Crib, Pinch, Rip, Trip, Truffle, and Tom! We shall *never* again meet in our innocent gambols, our rural sports, our fireside congratulations! These ideas might perhaps have shed a sorrowing gloom over my brightest anticipations, damped my energies, blighted my fondest hopes, and even led me, in some despairing moment, to commit dogicide or hydrophobia; but at the music of my master's voice my spirits revived; my whole frame throbbed with emotions of inexpressible delight when his gentle smile assured me of his continued confidence and friendship. All these farewell visits would not have aroused my suspicions; but when my old Tripey came, with her long and mournful whinings, clasping and hugging me to her bosom, and casting on me her "long and lingering looks," as she sad and homewards bent her way, I doubted somewhat the import of her redoubled caresses. Still more did I surmise, as the assembled household congregated around my master, sobbing their passage to the outer gate, where the recollection of our last parting rushed to my mind. But I felt no pang, I shed no tear. Strange that I should not grieve to part from those whom I ever loved to meet! that no anxious sigh or solitary throb should disturb this placid devotion to my master's will! Yes, we were to seek our fortunes in a far distant country; but to me all climates were genial, all lands happy and fair, where I might trace his footsteps or linger at his feet. As we were about to embark on board the ship that was to bear us from Liverpool to America, my master having paid his own passage, his next concern was to provide for his faithful Tiger. We went on board a few hours previous to our departure, when the mate announced to him, in rather a haughty, imperious tone, that no dog would be allowed on board. My master represented to him that I was a great favorite, perfectly quiet and inoffensive, and that rather than leave me to my fate, he would lose his own passage and take another ship; observing, moreover, that he would have no objection to pay any reasonable price rather than subject himself to that inconvenience. After a few arguments, the sum was agreed on and paid, and Tiger was to be transported to New-York on condition of his *never being seen on deck.* So I was shoved into a dark corner, both out of sight and out of hearing, which recalled to my mind all my little acts of disobedience, for some of which (I could not but imagine) I was now to suffer the penalty. But, I "spake not a word of sorrow," and as my master occasionally came to visit me, I imploringly besought him to release me, expressing to him (as best I could) my total unconsciousness of the cause of my imprisonment. I was well provided with food, but I felt really dejected and well-nigh hopeless.

However, my misery was of short duration. My master had besought the captain in my behalf, setting forth my wonderful developments, my long-tried fidelity, and my intrinsic worth; so exciting his curiosity that he became anxious to witness some of my performances. So Tiger was allowed, after three days' solitary confinement, to be presented on deck. On regaining my freedom my joy knew no bounds, as I felt satisfied my master had forgiven me and received me again into his favor. When the captain had witnessed some of my exploits of jumping, fetching, carrying, finding, my ups and downs, ins and outs, and with what wonderful alacrity and precision I executed all my master's commands, he kindly permitted me to remain on deck, providing that I did not interfere with the working of the ship or the comfort of the passengers. As in fine weather I was allowed the range of the vessel, I availed myself of the privilege to make a general investigation. I scarcely found one among that motley crowd of emigrants, but noticed me and appeared desirous of courting my acquaintance. The mass of them were indeed a rough-looking set, whose entry I might have well disputed had they presented themselves at my master's gate. I at first, therefore, looked on them with a suspicious eye, and even refused to respond to their overtures of friendship. But after a few days, I discovered that my fears were groundless, as I scarcely ever met with either annoyance or abuse, and Tiger was soon far better known than any other passenger on the ship. Though many of these rude specimens of expatriated rascality were continually warring and fighting among themselves, they never molested me, but often divided with me their scanty meals; nor were there more than two or three among them all that caused me any uneasiness, and *they* were not among those I had at first suspected; for I dreaded more a polished boot than a stout-nailed brogan. The ship being dreadfully infested with rats, I amused myself continually in hunting them out, and thereby succeeded in destroying great numbers: I sometimes came near stifling myself in the cargo, so impetuous was I in my researches. Once, indeed, I got so completely jammed in between the water-casks on deck, that without my having been delivered by the use of handspikes, I could never have extricated myself. We had a long and tedious passage: provisions became scarce, and water was dealt out to us in very minute doses; yet in the very face of half-starvation, I fattened on emigrating liberality and kindness, as few withheld from me a morsel of their contracted allowance, although my appearance was far from indicating emptiness or want. Besides all these constant contributions, my master provided me my regular meals, which I often had to refuse, from being overburdened with the considerations of my numerous friends. When I was thirsty, I would bark at the carpenter for water, and he really appeared to have more feeling for me, than for many of the Celtic unfortunates who pressed so eagerly around him. When the weather was fair, I was summoned on the quarter-deck, to divert the cabin passengers with my numerous feats. As usual on such occasions, various heavy sums of money were bid for me, but all respectfully rejected, as my kind master knew not where to procure such another Tiger. I occasionally visited also the sailors in the forecastle, who absolutely vied with each other in courting my friendship and good will. They were hard-looking fellows, but they treated me with the greatest tenderness and hospitality. I do not recollect any very remarkable incidents of the voyage. From day to day I followed the same routine. Hunting rats, visiting my acquaintances, performing occasionally a multitude of antics, waiting on the cook, and begging for water, were my principal occupations. But at night I lay at my master's feet, with watchful ear and sleepless eye, ready to arouse him in case of alarm and defend him in the hour of danger. But my defensive abilities were never called into action, as I reposed peacefully and he slept soundly. One thing I really did miss—there was not one of my own genus in the whole ship with whom I could divert myself, for I searched and searched in vain. How happy should I have felt if Trusty, Vick, or Manso had only been on board! What fun we should have had together! Poor old Truffle! I often thought of him, and should have been delighted to chat with him on our early freaks and adventures. But Johnny, though dead, still rises in my throat, harrowing up my latent passions, bidding me grasp the very shadow of his hairy pelt.

CHAPTER XXXVII.

TIGER ARRIVES SAFE IN NEW-YORK.—SUNDRY SKIRMISHES AND ANNOYANCES.

At last we arrived safe in New-York. As we landed on the dock, my first impression was, that I should be either choked to death with the heat or be eaten up piecemeal by flies. In this irritated state, before I had been five minutes on shore, I was attacked, without the least provocation, by a dirty-looking cur, twice my own size, who pounced on me, as though he intended to finish me off in a jiffy. But I took him by the fore-leg, and after giving him a few of my old-fashioned pinches, he limped off in a frightful hurry, demonstrating, at the same time, his heartfelt regret at having formed my acquaintance. During the few months we remained in the city of New-York, I was principally of service in warning off pedlers, beggars, and other interlopers, who were in the habit of walking up stairs and entering our apartments without knocking at the door. This annoyed us so much, that my master posted me on a mat at the head of the stairs, with strict orders to give due notice of the approach of strangers. This task I was thoroughly competent to. Thus our privacy was secured to us, as I allowed none, without permission, to enter our chambers. A *single* look of mine was sufficient to warn off all vagrants, as I had a peculiar way of showing my teeth, when I really had no intention of turning them to account. On the approach of a stranger, after giving him a specimen of my voice, I scratched at the door, as I considered myself bound to allow no one to come up without the presence of one of the inmates. But I was no cause of terror to those who presented themselves on legitimate business, provided they neither abused nor interrupted me when on guard. The person of the greatest unknown, when acknowledged by my master, was held sacred by me, and visitors, when in the house, I treated with the greatest possible civility. Nevertheless, even after repeated visits, I never allowed them to pass without giving them due notice to wait the arrival of my master or one of the family. On one or two occasions I recollect having been compelled to adopt severe measures. Once an impudent, determined Dutch pedler insisted on mounting the staircase, in spite of my threats. This I was bound to resist at all hazards. My warnings were ineffectual, as he not only attempted to force his passage, but threatened to dislodge me with one of his loaded baskets, which I immediately seized and tore out of his hands, and then grabbed him by the leg, upon which he hastily bolted down stairs, upsetting all his merchandize, and reeling headlong into the street. I merely pursued him to the entry-door, when my master (who had been in the garden) was disturbed by the rumpus, and hastened to recall me to my post. I had not materially injured the interloper, though he spluttered away for some time, and threatened to have his revenge. He never fulfilled his threats: perhaps he thought I had done no more than my duty, or rather feared lest his second visit might prove more unprofitable than the first. Dear me! how the fleas began to annoy me in New-York! I really thought they would drive me mad. I rolled and tumbled, tossed, whined, and fretted, and when I got into the water 't was ten times worse—they all bolted to my head to save themselves from drowning, and I feared they would absolutely poke my eyes out. As soon as my master discovered my distress, he rubbed something all over me, and in a few minutes I felt quite comfortable. What a pleasurable relief, to be sure! If our masters only knew what a horrid feeling it is to have, perhaps, a thousand mouths feasting at once on our irritated and tender pelts, they would never allow us to be aggravated, worried, and gnawed by such detestable vermin.

CHAPTER XXXVIII.

TIGER RELATES SUNDRY INCIDENTS AND ADVENTURES IN CITY AND COUNTRY.—HE EXTERMINATES HOGS AND CATS.

In traveling the city of New-York, I found the canines generally civil and well-behaved, except when they were backed and excited by rowdy boys, who delighted far more than *they* in snapping and snarling. One of these *loafers* undertook to take possession of me, one day, thinking, perhaps, that I was without a protector; but I immediately snapped his finger, upon which he hastily retired, cursing me to his heart's content. But I had no idea of changing masters in that way, and never allowed strangers to meddle with me in the street. A colored gentleman one day opened his umbrella at me, thinking to create a little sport for his lady, by witnessing my precipitate retreat. I was never born to run away, as I had never received any instruction on the subject. This novel mode of attack, therefore, so aggravated me that I tore his umbrella into ribbons, and was about to embrace one of his understandings, when my master requested me to desist. I always disliked to be pointed at, and although I never bit without sufficient provocation, I invariably threatened any who might undertake to insult me, considering myself entitled to common civility, even from strangers.

Not long after our arrival, we spent a few weeks in the neighborhood of the city, where our friends were greatly annoyed by the almost constant depredations of cattle and swine, who cared but little for the useless threats of the family watch-dog. I was appealed to and put on guard, and soon warned the invaders that my orders would be enforced to the letter. In a short time I had nearly rid the premises of these marauders, without having done them any serious injury, as they evidently considered me in earnest, and appeared greatly alarmed at my approach; a slight pinch or two having proved sufficient to convince them of my intentions. Nevertheless, one tusky old boar seemed willing to set me at defiance: although he had many times retreated without my handling him very severely, he still persisted in his daily inroads. This aggravated me greatly, it is true, yet I dared not, without the express commands of my master, resort to any sanguinary extremities. However, this audacious destroyer had been so long and ineffectually warned, pelted, hunted, and worried, that I was at last ordered to deal with him according to his deserts, and my master was requested to excite me to the attack. No sooner was the order given, than I rushed on him, seized him by the snout, and hung fast to him, till he began rolling to shake me off, upon which I caught him by the throat, and so kept him in subjection that he could not get possession of his legs; in fact, he seemed completely paralyzed, as I buried my teeth in his windpipe. A few minutes more and his accounts were for ever closed, had not my master arrived just in time to prevent me from converting him into pork. I need scarcely add, that his *boarship* was never seen within gunshot of the forbidden ground. With the exception of a few cats, who had devoured a host of young chickens, and were in the habit of disturbing the family repose by their nightly caterwauling, I had nothing further to attend to in that particular line of business. But their constant thefts and intrusions were unbearable; I was consequently commanded to annihilate them, the first favorable opportunity. I dispatched one, just as he was hurrying off with a fine young chicken in his mouth; the second I seized as he was sneaking along to get into the dairy, where he had been in the habit of saving the girl the trouble of skimming the milk. The family were all extremely gratified with my services, and presented me with a handsome collar. A more unwelcome present they never could have imagined, as I confess I was particularly averse to anything of the kind, and always did my utmost to convince my master of the fact, by exhibiting evident signs of joy and rejoicing whenever it was removed.

Everybody seemed to agree with Dick Marks and his friends, that I was a *good ún;* but, as I before observed, little did I foresee my future destiny, when he hurried off with me in his pocket.

CHAPTER XXXIX.

TIGER MOVES TO NEW-JERSEY.—ENCOUNTERS SNAKES, MUSK-RATS, AND SNAPPING-TURTLES.

But great was my rejoicing when we left the crowded city, and found ourselves in the land of turtles, snakes, and musk-rats in the woods of New-Jersey. As I had never seen any of this kind of game before, I was somewhat in doubt as to my course of action, particularly with regard to the former. I sometimes would carry one of the hard-coated mud-grubbing gentry for a mile, without even threatening him with an assault, as they all seemed perfectly harmless. But hard as were their shells, I have more than once gnawed my way through and dragged them out. I should never have acted thus toward these unoffending creatures, had I not been the subject of a most severe attack from a large snapping-turtle, who almost broke my leg in attempting to draw it into his capacious dwelling. On his loosening me I seized his protruding head, and in spite of the anguish which he occasioned me in endeavoring to shelter it from my menacing ivories, I succeeded in grinding it off before I relinquished my hold. I confess I was not over partial to such encounters, and should never have ventured, had I not been excited to the conflict. I had not been accustomed to contend with such iron-bound customers, and at first considered them perfectly impregnable. I had often killed hedgehogs, in spite of their thorny covering; and though my nose streamed with blood, my punishment only maddened me the more; but turtles I could not comprehend; consequently, I felt but little pleasure in reducing their fortresses, as I had to use up too much ammunition previous to effecting a breach, and even then was I dissatisfied with the plunder. As to snakes, I felt the utmost abhorrence of them: I really believe I never should have meddled with them at all, without orders. I had scarcely perfected myself in the art of destroying these disgusting pests, when circumstances occurred which induced my master to forbid me ever venturing to interfere with them again. Presto, my daughter, had at this period arrived at the age of maturity, and generally accompanied us in our rambles; but, notwithstanding she understood the management of these reptiles as well as I did, she received a bite in the tongue from one of the most venomous kind. On her return home, her throat and head were so enormously inflamed that she could take no manner of nourishment, became infuriated with agony and starvation, and died a raving maniac.

CHAPTER XL.

TIGER AND HIS DAUGHTER "PRESTO" IN CONSULTATION AND ACTION.

But pardon me! I am in advance of a history which I dare not close thus abruptly. My daughter Presto (although I say it myself) was the most amiable, pleasing, and intelligent companion I ever associated with, and I cannot but flatter myself that she was in a great measure indebted to me for her marvelously precocious developments. She was born within a few yards of my kennel, and never varied in her attachment to me, from the hour of our earliest acquaintance to the period of the sad catastrophe which terminated her career; and if ever I had cause to lament the demise of any of my canine friends, her loss to me was the most severe. As she associated with *me alone* from her earliest stage of pupdom, she became thoroughly initiated in all my acts and ways. In the daytime we were often allowed to ramble together where we pleased. We had wonderful sport, particularly among the musk-rats, which pleased us far more than any other recreation. It was sometimes a terrible job to get at them, as we had to gnaw off the roots of trees and bury ourselves in the mud, before we could seize on these amphibious delvers. We were indefatigable in our exertions, seldom retiring from the chase, before polishing our teeth on the scented carcasses of our prey. On our return from these expeditions, we were so disfigured with mud that our most intimate friends could never have recognized us. How admirably we worked together! so well versed were we in each other's movements, that rare indeed did anything escape us. As my daughter Presto was by far the fleeter of the two, she was generally foremost in the hunt. When she was tied up, I knew how to beg for her release, and made myself thoroughly understood; she also did the same in my behalf, whenever I was bound to my kennel. We invariably held a consultation together, previous to deciding on our route, and my master was greatly amused in witnessing our deliberations. When occasionally I felt disinclined for a distant ramble, I had to use all my eloquence to dissuade Presto from her determination and check her importunities. But as I, like her, was devotedly attached to the sport, she generally succeeded in clearing up my objections, and even in fascinating me to her will. When we took our meals off the same platter, to *her* I yielded the choicest morsels, and have often withdrawn rather than forfeit her good will and affection. At night we were never known to venture off, but kept incessant guard around the house and barns, barring all admission to strangers, and giving notice to all passers-by that Tiger and Presto were on duty. One little incident I can well remember, as having put us both to the test. Two men were bent on robbing our chicken-house, and were on the eve of commencing the work, when we both attacked them in the rear, and as they effected a precipitate flight, we indelibly printed our names on their legs and heels, and should easily have captured them had any one come to our assistance. The sound of my name was alone quite sufficient to warn the chickens from entering the garden, as they were accustomed to hear my name echoed whenever I had driven them out; so that even in my absence, the word Tiger was a sovereign antidote against all their aggressions.

CHAPTER XLI.

TIGER AND "PRESTO" EXECUTE JUDGMENT ON A TRAITOR.

We were on the most intimate terms with the cat, who often messed with us and even visited our kennels, without the least fear of annoyance. Little did I think it would ever fall to our lot to visit her with the severest penalty of the law. As the rats were accused of carrying off nightly a portion of the early chickens that were kept in the kitchen, the cat was carefully shut in with them, to protect them from their attacks. In the morning their number seemed to have still decreased, and Puss was set down as worthless; but when the shattered remnants of their bones and feathers were found in her hiding-place, she herself was rightly adjudged to be the murderess. Therefore she was justly condemned to die, and to Tiger and Presto was allotted the task of putting the judgment into execution. She was brought out, and great was our surprise when the command was issued. We both doubted for a moment, presuming it to be a joke; but on the order being repeated, we set to the work, Presto taking one end and I the other, till Puss was fairly rent asunder. She heartily deserved an ignominious death, although we were both unwilling to be her executioners. For my part, I never could place confidence in cats, although I have had some rather agreeable acquaintances of the feline tribe. I always think of old Tom, who invariably deserted his mistress in the hour of peril, while Truffle and I remained faithful by her side. I felt lonely indeed, after poor Presto's untimely death, and many weeks passed away before I could reconcile myself to the bereavement.

CHAPTER XLII.

TIGER'S SON AND PUPIL "LION."—HIS PRECOCIOUS COURAGE AND EXPANDING INTELLECT.—DARING ADVENTURES AND DEATH.

My son Lion, now only a few weeks old, was rather an annoyance to me than otherwise, as he was apt to intrude himself on me when I was little inclined for mirth. But I knew not how to be angry with him, although he occasionally somewhat ruffled my temper. He had only reached his tenth week, when his youthful pluck was put to the most extraordinary test. We were returning from a visit to a neighboring town, and as my son Lion was yet too young to travel far on foot, he was riding with my master in the wagon, while I was running on some distance ahead. He suddenly dashed out of my master's arms, jumped off the wagon, crossed the ditch, hurrying into an adjoining swamp, where he immediately engaged in mortal combat with an enormous musk-rat. This encounter had lasted some minutes, (and a bloody conflict it was,) when I was attracted by the squeaking, and returned to ascertain the cause. What was my surprise on witnessing my dauntless offset struggling valiantly with his relentless foe! I trembled for the result, and sprang on his adversary, dealing him instantaneous death. I regret having been too hasty, as I have every reason to believe my little Lion would have polished him off without my interference. My master was exceedingly disappointed at my appearance, and recalled me, when it was too late. Nevertheless, I allowed Lion to enjoy all the glory of the victory, and he could not be persuaded to slacken his grasp on the bloody corpse, which convinced me that he was still eager for the fight, regardless of the severity of his own wounds. Such a trial of precocious pluck would have daunted many a chicken-hearted mongrel; but I would not acknowledge even a second cousin of mine who would flinch in the hour of peril, and disgrace the name of Tiger.

This was surely an early introduction to a train of noble feats, which, instead of impregnating him with fear, rendered him absolutely reckless of danger and death. Not many months elapsed, before he fully supplied the vacancy occasioned by the demise of my worthy daughter Presto. Although I now began to feel somewhat the stiffness of old age, I was still firm and hardy, and as capable as ever of a hard day's work. With Lion I hunted the forest, as in former days, equally enjoying the sport and glorying in success, and I am satisfied that my son was far more indebted to me for my example, than to all his other teachings. Whatever he saw me do, he did the same. If I barked, he barked too; if I lay down, he stretched himself out too; when I was ordered away, he followed suit; when I was called, he generally answered first; whatever I attacked, he was bound to seize; if I wagged my tail, his was immediately set in motion. In fine, every one said he was exactly like *me*. No wonder—he copied me in everything; dogged after me wherever I traveled, howling like a boneless mongrel if I absented myself but a moment from his sight. In fact, I was quite as delighted with his company, as he was inconsolable in my absence. He was more quarrelsome than I ever was, which led him into many serious scrapes. Before he was a year old, he took the liberty of slaughtering a neighboring dog, who entered our yard in pursuit of a chicken. Whether this was to satisfy his pugnacious temperament, or to rid the premises of an ill-bred interloper, is not for me to determine. I am rather inclined to believe he delighted in exercising his powers, though I must say I never saw him attack his inferiors in size: on the contrary, he was too venturesome in challenging canines of heavier metal than himself. True, he was but young, and, had his life been spared, he would no doubt (like myself) have acquired wisdom by experience, and have more fully profited by his early lessons, eminently calculated to moderate his impetuous temper and restrain his stubborn will.

Never was a more faithful guard. Anything intrusted to him was perfectly safe in his keeping. The weather was raging hot, when my master once laid down his coat in the wood, bidding him take charge of it; and as we were afterwards engaged at some distance off, Lion chanced to be forgotten for several hours. I was ordered to look after him; and as I started off in the direction where he was left, it recalled to my master's recollection his having left him in charge of the coat. On arriving at the spot, we found him faithful to his trust, but elated beyond measure at his deliverance, as he testified a joyful pride at having executed his master's will. He seemed perfectly willing to allow anything to be brought on the premises, but nothing could go off without a passport from one of the family. I shall never forget the sport he had with a large Billy-goat, who chanced to wander into our yard. It was the first he had ever seen, and when he was ordered to the attack he very carefully surveyed him all over; after which he saluted him with a threatening bark, upon which Mr. Billy sent him reeling with one of his favorite butts, then stamped in proud defiance, daring him to return to the charge. I fully expected that I should have been commanded to the attack, but my son Lion, far from being daunted, (though somewhat stupified with the blow,) was soon on his legs, and eager to provoke the combat. He rushed into him, seized him by the nose, and held him in abeyance. There stood Billy, motionless, powerless, except in speech, uttering the most pitiful and imploring cries I had ever heard, and (as I thought) begging hard for his life. But my son was so exceedingly irritated by this unexpected attack, that I believe he would have retained his prisoner until sunset. My master, however, presuming that Billy's first lesson might deter him from any further aggressions, ordered Lion to release him, to which he very reluctantly assented. On feeling himself at liberty, Billy hastily sprang over the fence without touching a rail, no doubt with the fixed determination of never retracing his steps. Just as I thought—he never *did* enter our premises again. When he passed that way he was always observed to slip hastily by, on the opposite side of the road. The day after this occurrence, we both met him at some distance from the house, when I fully expected my son would have sought his revenge. What was my astonishment, as he coolly examined him from stem to stern, bidding him pursue his course in peace.

Lion (like my daughter Presto) had imbibed a deeply-rooted aversion to all kinds of snakes. I had long ceased to meddle with them, as I had received positive orders not to molest them any further. But *he* seemed to take the greatest delight in their destruction, and often wondered why I should remain a passive spectator of such an exhilirating pastime. I cannot say how it happened, but one fine summer's day, as we were on our way to the musk-rat depôt, Lion, the fearless Lion, was bitten on the muzzle by a venomous serpent. On our arriving at the hunting-ground he refused to join in the sport, and we returned hastily home. My master observed a strangeness in his expression, and chained him fast to the kennel. The next day I noted myself a certain wildness in his eye, his very glance forbidding my approach, while his throat was so inflamed that his breathing was somewhat difficult, and he refused all nourishment, with the exception of milk. The next day he appeared worse. A choice young Charley spaniel, with whom he was previously on the most intimate terms, chanced to approach within the reach of his chain, upon which the infuriated Lion sprang on him, seized him, carried him into his house, grinding and masticating him into a perfect pulp. This act convinced us at once that my poor Lion was raving mad. In this state he remained for several days, when my master, seeing there were no hopes of his recovery, and fearing lest any of us might become a prey to his ungovernable fury, determined on putting him out of his misery. In order to effect this in the most speedy and merciful way, he approached his kennel, just beyond the reach of his chain, still hoping he might evince some favorable symptom of returning consciousness. But on presenting a stick to him, he furiously grasped it, unaffected by either entreaty or remonstrance, and upon that being withdrawn, sprang at my master in frantic rage, still baying and threatening him at his chain's length, when, with one "fell swoop" from a sharp hatchet, his head was split in twain, and a momentary struggle terminated his existence. I was extremely anxious to make a post-mortem examination, but was peremptorily forbidden. Even when he reposed deep in the earth, I was strongly tempted to exhume the body. This satisfaction was also denied me. I therefore concluded to let him alone. Poor fellow! we all grieved over his untimely end. Had he lived, he might have been a great comfort to me in my old years, and at my demise have rendered himself worthy of that confidence which my master had so long and justly reposed in me.

CHAPTER XLIII.

TIGER AGAIN VICTORIOUS.—TRAGICO-COMIC ENCOUNTER WITH SCHLACHTENMEISTER'S FIVE WONDERFUL CATS.

I am now getting to be what some would call an old dog. But I had a good strong constitution, and I never abused it, although I have gone through many *hard rubs;* but as I was rough and hardy, and had a good friend to nurse me in all my afflictions, I was not to be cut off until I had run out the natural measure of my days. I recollect, in my younger days, having had two or three narrow escapes of my life. I was once engaged in a trivial conversation with a canine acquaintance, when a cart, heavily laden, passed over my body. I was then set down as past all recovery, and even pronounced dead: doubtless I should soon have breathed my last, but my master, who had selected me as his companion, attended me with such devoted perseverance that I was speedily restored to perfect health. But I have not yet quite exhausted the theme of my own adventures. Among the queerest was the following: As I have frequently observed,

I never interfered with anything, unless acting under my master's orders. I therefore was often compelled to brook a variety of insults. Had I been left to follow the dictates of my own naturally irritable disposition, I should no doubt have fallen an early prey to my inferior passions, and *might never have survived to chronicle my history after my death.* I was continually subject to attacks from cats, especially when any of the females chanced to be surrounded by a family. Many a score times have I longed for permission to resent their unprovoked and annoying assaults, but seldom indeed was I authorized to gratify my revenge. But there dwelt, on the high-road to the town nearest our residence, a certain man, who prided himself in the size and beauty of his five cats. What pleased him most, was to stand at his door, with his thumbs in his vest-pockets, witnessing their wonderful exploits. Such were his exalted ideas of his feline pets, that he pronounced them to be far superior, both in physical and mental endowments, to all the hairy quadrupeds in creation. They didn't eat like other cats, and never omitted to wash their faces after meals. He talked to them a great deal, and always in Dutch, firmly believing they digested every word of it. As he was an old bachelor, they all slept in bed with him, and (most miraculous to relate) they got up with him regularly in the morning, and surrounded his table at every meal: when he snored, they all snored too; and what is more, they waited regularly the arrival of the butcher, who dared not present himself at the porch without their wonted allowance of cats' meat. More marvelous still was their noted antipathy to all barking quadrupeds. With what fond delight did Herr Schlachtenmeister witness their attacks on well-nigh every unfortunate mongrel who dared unwittingly to approach that feline emporium! Tiger—yes, Tiger himself has many a time been the subject and object of their hated embraces, and has as often ignobly fled from their audacious, unprovoked assaults, reluctantly yielding to the dictates of education, rather than to a well-merited revenge.

But one day, as I was peacefully trotting along by my master's side, the whole fraternity, it appears, had resolved on a combined assault, as they simultaneously saluted me, face, back, and ribs, digging their claws into me as though they intended slicing me up for sourcrout. On witnessing this glorious tragedy, old Schlachtenmeister was convulsed with laughter. I was burning with revenge, and my master felt somewhat humiliated by the jeers of the passers-by. But it would still have gone off as a joke, if the elated cat-owner had failed to hint at my cowardice and retreating propensities, which at once decided my protector to back *me alone* to contend against his whole family united. "I tell you dey kill em in two minute; dey trive all de tam tog from mine house. Your tog no kill vun in vun veek." These and a few other vain-glorious remarks of the worthy Schlachtenmeister were uttered in a somewhat pitiful, yet defiant tone, and were speedily responded to by my master's offering to stake a five-dollar bill that *I alone* would put them all to flight in less than two minutes, excepting any that I might render incompetent to retreat. The money was posted in the hands of a third party. The conditions were agreed on. The combat was to take place on the day following, in the largest room in Schlachtenmeister's house, when only a few private friends were to be present. At the appointed hour we were all at the place of rendezvous, both sides mutually confident of success. As we entered, Schlachtenmeister saluted my master with a significant nodding smile, confirming his self-assurance by an indignant sarcastic grin at my person, at the same time remarking that "he tink de tog never vant no more shupper." My master merely requested him not to be too hasty in his opinions, intimating that he had traveled a great deal, and had never yet heard of a cat annihilating a dog. The preliminary remarks were closed by Schlachtenmeister's sensible ultimatum—"Vell, vell; you'll shee, you'll shee." But now to the conflict. Schlachtenmeister first entered the arena with his favorites, at the same time bobbing his friend and giving him a knowing wink. It was arranged that at a given signal I should enter the room with my master, and immediately open the proceedings. I was at that time perfectly unconscious of the object of our visit; in fact, I felt rather nervous, expecting every moment that those velvet-pawed imps would be again exercising their claws on my defenceless pelt: I therefore kept rolling my eyes about in all directions, carefully scrutinizing every stool, chair, and table, as I kept close to my master's heels. But when he took me up and whispered to me a few well-known old-fashioned exciting ejaculations, I felt assured that my services were to be called in question. I struggled to spring from his arms, feeling myself doubly nerved with the idea that *now* I was to wreak my bursting vengeance on the objects of my utmost abhorrence.

What had I to fear from cats! I had encountered too many not to be fully conversant with their tactics. I knew the extent of their powers, as they had often done their utmost against me; but with all their tearing, pinching, and scratching, the only impression they ever made on me, was that the more they punished me, the sooner they repented it. As to putting *my* eyes out, as they have served many of my ignorant fellows, I always took good care to shut them after I had fixed on the point of my attack; and although many a time I have at once felt their fore-claws in my neck, their hind ones in my breast, and their teeth clenched in my cheek, I heeded it not, while at the same time I held them in my death-grasp, from which not one ever lived to escape. No, no: I was evidently not born to be the victim of catophobia. I would have died a hundred deaths, rather than succumb to such dastardly, faithless, hypocritical adversaries. But my master soon opened the door, when, at his well-known command, I instantaneously rushed into the *catty conclave*, seizing the first by the loins and giving him a hearty shake, while two more were burying their teeth and claws in my back: a fourth sprang on the mantlepiece, upsetting the china ornaments into the fireplace; while the fifth bolted through one of the upper squares of glass, and forced his way into the garden. I soon relaxed my first hold, to attend to my *back-friends*, grabbing one between the fore-legs, causing him to raise the most excruciating caterwauling. All this time poor Schlachtenmeister showed symptoms of heart-rending distress. "Och! mein Cot! mein Cot! he make dem all ted! he make dem all ted! I give you ten tollar you take him off! Donder and blitzen! I never see such von teufel of a tog!" But I was so much engaged executing my master's orders to the letter. "Kill him, Tiger! Shake him, Tiger! Good dog, Tiger!" Two were already sprawling apparently in the agonies of death, when a third, to escape my wrath, had concealed all his weapons in Schlachtenmeister's neck and arms, and as I was attempting to dislodge him, his affrighted owner begged loud for mercy; "Take him vay! take him vay! mein Cot! mein Cot! tat tam tog keel me!" His personal fears were perfectly groundless, as my orders referred simply to his cats, and he was speedily indebted to me for delivering him from his unenviable predicament, as I impetuously dislodged the third from her hopeless shelter. His prayers, promises, and intreaties at last induced my master to request me to relinquish the fight.

Behold now the field of battle! Two magnificent cats lying helpless and hopeless; a third limping off to the nearest hiding-place; a fourth suddenly concealed by Schlachtenmeister in the bureau-drawer; while the fifth had succeeded, uninjured, in effecting his exit. Next, cast your eyes on the chopfallen cat-master, writhing from torture inflicted on him by one of his *own favorites*, viewing with affrighted astonishment his shattered ornaments, bloody carpet, and expiring pets; and hear him exclaim, "Sush von tog! Sush von tog!" Witness the satisfactory smile of my protector, as he exultingly administers to me the well-known pat of victory, at the same time pocketing the stakes. Above all, just look at me! A few insignificant digs, narrow scratches, and small streaks of blood, are my only emblems of conflict; which have but tended to brighten my eye, enliven my spirits, and goad me on to acts of renewed valor and daring.

My only cause of regret was, that I was not allowed to finish off the whole company of caterwaulers, from whose treacherous assaults I had so often unwillingly retreated. As it was, I had sufficient cause of inward satisfaction, not only from the immediate result of the engagement, but from its consequences. One of my foes breathed his last previous to our quitting the ground; a second survived only a few days; a third recovered after a little nursing; the fourth had remained ensconced and was uninjured: but the fifth (who was, of course, devotedly attached to his doting Schlaehtenmeister) was never known to re-enter his dwelling. The remaining two were seldom again observed to visit the road-side of the house; and when they perchance caught sight of old Tiger as he passed that way, they invariably descended from inside the kitchen window, to seek refuge in obscurity. Great as was the disappointment of Schlachtenmeister at the wind-up of this fatal skirmish, still I must do him the credit to mention, that he failed not ever after to extol me in the highest terms, and openly to confess that "sush von tog" was worth more than all the cats from the North Pole to the Equator. He begged my master to spare him one of my sons, for which he would be perfectly willing to pay a *good price;* at the same time observing that he should then get rid of the balance of his cats, convinced as he was of their selfishness and treachery, and adopt my son as his guardian and companion.

CHAPTER XLIV.

TIGER LOSES HIS MASTER IN THE CITY OF NEW-YORK.—AFTER FRUITLESS RESEARCHES, HE TAKES THE BOAT FOR NEW-JERSEY.

Once, when I accompanied my master to the city of New-York, I unfortunately lost sight of him, as he passed through into the opposite street, by a door which we had not entered. I followed pretty close upon him, but the door slammed to before I reached it. I concluded that he intended to return for me, although I felt somewhat uneasy among strangers. Having waited for some time, I made up my mind at once to go in search of him, and, slipping off, I hastily visited every place I had known him to frequent. I tracked him through every street we had passed. Indeed, I became so excited in pursuit of him, that I became jaded and thirsty. I would gladly have screened myself from the effects of the scorching sun, and cooled my dripping tongue, but I dared not make friends with any one, as I was strongly suspicious of being detained. Many were the insults heaped upon me as I fretted my way backward and forward; for, instead of relieving my distress, I was hooted at, and even pelted by many, who might have easily imagined the cause of my excitement. Finding all my researches vain, I determined on returning to the pier where we had landed, thinking my master might be expecting me there. But he had alike sought me ineffectually, and, quite unknown to me, returned to his home (eighteen miles distant.) I considered that my better plan would be to take the next boat, which would land me within a few miles of my destination. I waited patiently on the pier till the boat arrived, during which time I was very politely accosted by several ragged urchins, some of whom endeavored to entice me with food, others to ornament me with a string or collar. But on their approaches I made a few threatening grimaces, causing them to forego their praiseworthy attempts of taking charge of me. On the arrival of the boat I sprang on board the first, and immediately searched the cabins through and through, thinking perhaps to discover some traces of my master, but without success. I doubted for a moment whether to return or continue my researches in the city, but soon decided on the former, as it was now growing late, and I naturally supposed my master must have returned home. The boat was crowded with people, several of whom recognized me and treated me with corresponding respect. I paid some slight attention to the favorable notice they took of me; but, fearing too great an intimacy, I kept myself as distant as possible. Some of the passengers proposed taking charge of me, to deliver me in safety to my master, and were about placing a cord around my neck to insure my safety; nevertheless, my resistance was so threatening and determined, that I was allowed to take my chance. Depend on it, I was the first passenger that landed, and away I posted, straining every nerve to put an end to my almost despairing anxiety. But I was scarcely out of sight of the boat, when, to my great surprise, I came in contact with my master, who, not finding me at home, as he had suspected, was coming to make inquiries concerning me; and I really believe the inexpressible joy I felt at his recovery more than atoned for all the misery I had endured from the dreaded idea of never meeting him again. One might have presumed I had been absent six months, to judge from our repeated congratulations. Every word he uttered caused me to spring with delight: my fatigues were all forgotten; and although I felt somewhat ashamed at having lost sight of my benefactor, his gentle upbraidings only added to my raptures, and bid me redouble my efforts of gratitude and obedience. I was indeed of far more value to him than I could be to a stranger, as he knew all my ways, my virtues, and defects. I had grown up under his discipline, and never transgressed against him without a feeling of remorse. I needed no chastisement to enforce his will, as to indulge it was the pride of my life. I desired no reward for watching his interests, for to protect them was the sole object of my existence. I might perchance have done my duty in other hands, but could never have lavished on another such disinterested and unwavering devotion. My eyes, ears, and voice—aye, my very feet and tail, revealed to him the language of my heart. Well could he discern, by their varied motions, my every want, desire, and inclination, so expressively conveyed by their eloquent and truthful meanderings.

CHAPTER XLV.

"TIPPO," THE CELEBRATED POODLE, SUCCUMBS TO TIGER'S SUPERIOR COURAGE AND SKILL.

But I have now to record an aquatic feat, which, though it commenced in sport, bore every indication of a tragic termination. As I have before observed, my master placed unlimited confidence in my abilities. This led him often to declare that I was *cut out* for all emergencies, and would shrink from nothing. A certain well-known gent owned one of the most remarkable poodles in existence. Water was his favorite element: there he swam like a fish, dived like a duck, and floated like a cork. His master had given many fruitless challenges to all who dared to extol the merits of Newfoundland, spaniel, or poodle, little dreaming that his big woolly poodle would ever be outwitted by my comparatively insignificant bull-terrier personage. The match was simple; the stakes were small, but Tiger was bound to win them all. I had been long acquainted with my opponent, and had always been on the best of terms with his woolly dogship. He was not naturally of a pugnacious temperament, and as I had been taught to control my natural pride and susceptibility, we had never had the most trifling disagreement. Having continually practiced for years my swimming and diving powers, in seas, lakes, rivers, canals, and brooks, I felt myself perfectly at home, either in navigating an ocean or fathoming a mud-puddle. No task but I must undertake, no obstacle but I must overcome. My inborn pluck, my superior education and devotion to my protector, urged me onward to deeds of daring and valor, thus working out the most unmistakable epithet to the honored memories of the invincible Don and the matchless Vixen.

But the owner of Tippo, the celebrated poodle, affirmed and contended that his amphibious barker would fetch anything out of the water before any other canine in dogdom. This my master stoutly denied, and even offered to stake my very person on the result of a match, although he would not have bartered me for all the poodles in New-Jersey. In fine, the match was made, and the stakes posted on the bank of the river, in trust of one of the bystanders. A stick was to be thrown as far as possible into the water by a third party, and he that brought it ashore was to be declared the winner. Great was the excitement. Betting was considerably in favor of the poodle, as he was declared to be a *real water-dog*. The word was given—" One," " Two," " Three," and away flew the stick some thirty or forty yards from the shore. As we were both jumping up, anxious to seize it before the signal was given, the start was instantaneous; but as I had been so thoroughly versed in springing after water-rats, I was bound to take the lead in all adventures of this kind. I sprang like a Tiger, keeping ahead of my opponent, whose disappointed growlings threatened me in the rear. I was rather surprised at the unpleasant observations he was making, but my prize was onward. I hastened to grasp it, and scarcely succeeded in taking possession, when Tippo abruptly snatched it from me, upon which my master loudly commanded me to regain it at all hazards. I scarcely required such a recommendation, but immediately grabbed Mr. Tippo by the throat, and down we went together. 'T was not the first time the water had covered me. No: I had often traveled beneath its surface, rising only to regain my breath or to seek my prey. However, we soon rose again together, while I still made good my hold. No sooner had I recovered my wind than down I forced him again. As we were acting this aquatic tragedy, the safety of the poodle was being seriously discussed on shore. His master was exceedingly fearful of the result of our subaqueous manœuvreings, remarking that he really began to dread lest I should succeed in drowning his darling Tippo, upon which my ever-confident backer offered to stake ten dollars that Mr. Poodle would be a *goner* in less than ten minutes. This decided and well-grounded opinion so alarmed the protector of the drowning Tippo, that his master volunteered a considerable sum for his rescue. I was seriously bent on filling him with cold water, when, as we rose for the fifth or sixth time, I heard my master's voice imperiously commanding me to withdraw. As I was unhurt, and my antagonist well-nigh exhausted, I immediately released him and grasped the prize for which I was so earnestly contending, bearing it in triumph to my master's feet. Tippo reached the land with great difficulty, where he lay, on the opposite shore, half extinguished from suffocation and fright. On his recovering the use of his limbs he made tracks in the opposite direction, and in spite of the earnest entreaties of his disappointed guardian, succeeded in crossing the bridge, and arriving (*to his great astonishment*) at his canine domicil. In his hasty and suspicious retreat he kept continually glancing in the rear, no doubt dreading my approach. But I owed him no malice. Had he not interrupted me in my duty, my wrath would not have been kindled against him. The upshot of this encounter caused the whole company of spectators again to decide that I was a *good 'un.* A few days after, I met friend Tippo, and although he appeared to respond rather bashfully to my usual salutations, I soon succeeded in convincing him of my cordial forgiveness, and our intimacy was renewed on its former basis. We often met on shore, but were never known to bathe in sight of each other, as Tippo invariably selected a circuitous route homeward, rather than risk the shadow of a second aquatic diversion with the indomitable Tiger. Poor fellow! I dare say he was a most excellent *poodle;* and as little was expected of him, he gave universal satisfaction.

I could never see much to admire in poodles. They are too sheepy in their manners and coats to please me: neither fighters, rat-catchers, nor hunters; poor guardians, helpless friends, and ridiculous enemies. True, they could acquire many fancy tricks, and create some little amusement, but their powers were too insignificant to be turned to any serviceable account. Nevertheless, I must not make enviable contrasts, or disparage others to exalt myself. If they please their masters, that is all that ought to be required of them. Still more, if they delight the ladies, they can boast of that to which few of my own class have ever aspired, as females are seldom struck with our beauty or pleased with our natural propensities.

CHAPTER XLVI.

TIGER GIVES A WONDERFUL ACCOUNT OF HIS PUPIL "NERO."

Nero! Nero! Companion of my waning years! Guardian of my toothless dogship! Thanks to thy more than brotherly affection, I was not left in the decline of life to mourn my departing strength, to grieve over my tenantless gums, or to pine at the closing scenes of a pleasurable and active career, faithfully devoted to the most deserving of protectors! As I have often remarked, I had many canine acquaintances, and several worthy, indeed, of my unrestricted intercourse and friendship, although I had been but slightly indebted to any of them for disinterested services they might have rendered me. Notwithstanding our having afforded each other mutual sport, fun, and pastime, which was perhaps necessary to initiate us into the scenes of town and city travel, to fit us for the woodland hunt, the mountain range, or the prairie chase; to rid us of our bashful, vociferous, and doubting propensities, and convince us that even dogs, without a respectable share of boldness and impudence, are neither calculated to help themselves or protect their masters; yet, in all our varied associations, there generally existed a feeling of selfishness which occasionally marred our highest flights of enjoyment, and sometimes terminated our most friendly meetings in hasty and snappish adjournments. The noble Nero was more akin to my father's blood, though, to the best of my knowledge, not related to either of us. To a stranger his outward appearance was repulsive in the extreme, though in form and symmetrical proportions none had ever excelled him. His mother was born in Dublin, his father in Warwick, England, while *he* first saw the light within the immediate sound of New-Jersey bull-frogs, catydids, tree-toads, and musketos. His parents were both of as pure bull-stock as the Old Country could furnish, of well-tried pluck and immeasurable daring. Alas! I am sorry to avow it, these were the only qualities of which they could boast, or rather of which they had no reason to be proud. These were the unimproved gifts of nature, which, if duly restrained and well directed, might have rendered them matchless guardians and faithful companions. None dared to boast of their friendship, while all dreaded them as enemies. Uncertain in their affections, indiscriminating in their antipathies, their names were honored alone by dog-fighters and bullies. His father was a smooth-coated brindle bull-dog, with the most horrid-looking phiz that was ever exhibited to the public: large staring eyes, high forehead, short nose, and projecting under jaw, displaying in full his weapons of assault and defence, accompanied by a daring grin, which debarred all visitors from courting his acquaintance. Of his valor he bore undoubted marks. Two of his ribs were stove in by a bull, one of his legs was broken by a bear, while his indented scalp bore evident traces of hard-fought battles, in one of which his right ear was gnawed off, close to the skull. Certainly there was nothing prepossessing in his appearance, except his dread-nought, dare-devil expression; and as he was thoroughly tutored in the sublime art of seizing, lacerating, and destroying, his life was devoted to the unlimited exercise of his ungovernable passions. His mother was of a similar class: about his equal in size, and displaying equal purity of blood. She was the property of an Irishman, who prided himself in her ferocity even more than in his own. He had every reason to glory in it, as she was as ferocious as a hyena; so much so, that the near-dwellers, who greatly feared lest she might break loose and slake her fury on some innocent object, decided, one day, during the absence of her master, on ridding themselves of her dreaded attacks. Thus terminated the career of the mother of one of the best of quadrupeds that ever was trained by dog and man.

I should not thus have wandered from my own personal history and immediate connections, were it not simply to prove how often those of my own particular class are the objects of scorn and abuse, who might, but for man's culpable neglect, have proved themselves the noblest, the bravest, and the best. My pupil Nero was worthy of higher praises than I am eloquent enough to bestow on him, and principally to me was he indebted for his almost human understanding. At the age of four weeks my master delivered him into my peculiar charge. I was at first rather struck with his strange appearance and *hard* expression. He certainly did look like a *hard 'un*, and in some senses he was exactly so—hard to be convinced against his will, hard even to persuade, but true to all his professions and sincere in all his acts. He often witnessed my performances, and his ambition in imitating *me* was wonderful to witness. He looked to me for every movement, often inviting me to action when I was more inclined for repose. If I barked, he barked; and when he chanced to give the first alarm, he immediately ceased unless I seconded him. A look from me delayed his attacks or hastened his assaults; and as age gradually stiffened my limbs, dimmed my sight, and thickened my hearing, he was ever ready and willing to become my substitute; and although my strength and activity were fast declining, I never knew him take advantage of my weakness, or seriously threaten me with a display of his superior powers. He equally profited by what I refused to do, as he did by the example of my performances. Slow and hesitating were his first movements, until assured of my approval, when he was terrible in the assault and resistless in the defence. Such was his natural impetuosity, that all objects of attack to him were alike; and, knowing no fear, (without the dictates of my ripened judgment and discretion,) he would have become an early prey to his untutored passions. I do not wish to claim *all* the merits of his extraordinary instinctive and educational performances, as they were greatly enhanced and his perversities much restricted by my master's frequent trainings, in which I invariably assisted; but as he was seldom out of my sight, and ever guided by my example, he had opportunities of which but few could boast, of cultivating a native worth, in which few indeed were born his equals. These were not the sole qualifications which endeared him to my warmest affections. His unwavering attachment to me, at a period when my receding powers debarred me from affording him any reciprocal gratifications, his child-like obedience to my very nod, and his kindly consideration for my age and infirmities, rendered him (next to my own master) the object of my highest esteem and affection. My protector was also greatly delighted with Nero's expanding genius and almost intellectual qualifications, for which he awarded me a credit far beyond my deserts.

We are said to be very jealous animals, and we really are, I must admit. I *did* occasionally feel a jealous pang as my master praised my smiling pupil, and I have sometimes thought myself neglected as his name was echoed above my own. But there never once existed within me a feeling of bitterness against the worthy Nero or our mutual protector. A thought would sometimes arise within me, that I was growing aged and useless, a burden to myself and a profitless pensioner on my master's bounty. I could no longer expect refreshing rewards in consideration of my frequent services. My stiffened gait now forbade the wonted frolic; my vision, now bedimmed, had curtailed the pleasure of the chase; and my hearing, dull, detracted from my noted watchfulness; and although I somewhat begrudged Nero his caresses, and felt saddened that I could no longer merit my master's constant smile and approbation, yet I had constant proofs that, far from being cast off or neglected, I was still the admired and petted, though somewhat useless Tiger. I was still the senior and pattern of the four-legged department, respected and honored for what I had been, revered and consulted for what I was—an old experienced philosopher and friend No: how could a spark of enmity be engendered in me toward my guardian Nero? he who not only had never offended me, but who rendered me every service in his power, for which he was now declared Vice-President of the whole canine establishment. Who, on viewing his monster eyes and grim visage, could have divined them the index of such a noble, enlightened *mind*, and affectionate and loving heart. As he was a scholar principally of my own creation, I feel a pride in acknowledging that he was, in many respects, my equal, and in some, indeed, my superior. Truffle never taught me much, as he neither commanded my respect by his firmness, nor ensured my attention by his talents. Our natural powers are so seldom cultivated to their full extent, the majority of us being given over entirely to self-instruction, that even those who have been denied every advantage are stamped as incapable and worthless. True, nature has instinctively provided us with all that is necessary for our support and protection in our originally wild and untutored state; but if we are to be the companions of man, we require his teachings, to be wedded to his ways, to minister to his wants, and execute his commands. Far better, then, were it to smother, drown, or hang us at our birth, than force us into a society for which we are never to be fitted. Either give us an exit from a scornful world, or teach us to fill a station worthy of our domesticated capacity.

Nero began early to reason for himself. Once, I remember well, before he had been personally taught to find anything that was lost, he found a small tin pail, which had been carelessly left in the garden. I watched him take it carefully by the handle, and, often casting me a knowing look, he trotted off to the house, the outside door of which was open. Contrary to his orders he marched in, and passed on to the door of the sitting-room, where he waited some little time. Finding that no one came, he began knocking at the door. It was opened, and great was the surprise of the inmates as the young Nero stood with the pail in his mouth, fairly shaking it with delight. But when it was taken from him, his joy knew no bounds—his first effort was crowned with success. Had he been presented with a supply of food after a forty-eight hours' fast, his spirits could not have risen to a higher state of excitement. Proof of this was not long wanting, as the next morning he again presented himself at the door with another trophy of his dawning *reason*, and ever afterward he was constant in his researches, faithful and prompt in the restoration of whatever article he knew to be missing. Should anything threaten in the night, he never failed to arouse me, except in cases of sudden emergency, when he invariably decided to act on his own responsibility.

One night he had already caught a man getting over the fence into the garden, and I was aroused only by the cries of the detected thief, whom Nero had secured, and *there* he held him till my master arrived; but, contrary to my expectations, he had not lacerated him any further than was necessary to prevent his escape. He was, indeed, mild and gentle, though firm and decided. In all cases of seizure he invariably suited the pressure of his teeth to the obstinacy of his prisoner, whom he never released until delivered to safe custody. Perhaps he detained many honest men; but if he did, none of that stamp had occasion to fear him, as he never punished any that entered by the lawful way, merely arresting or safely accompanying them, till further orders. He was much larger and stronger than myself, his weight being over forty pounds, while I seldom exceeded twenty-eight. I began to get more irritable in my latter days, and got into more scrapes than usual on that account. As my powers were lessening, I was no longer capable of resisting foes, which I never feared to attack; but my true and sturdy friend Nero was ever ready to rush to my assistance and deliver me in the moment of peril. Many a time has he saved me from destruction, and was never so delighted as when rendering me assistance. Verily, the *tables were now turned.* He had *formerly* looked up to me for advice and support; *now* he was daily endeavoring to rid himself of his debt of gratitude, which enabled me to live out my old years in peace and retirement, enjoying to the last that repose which he was ever anxious to insure me.

I could relate a hundred of his sagaciously intellectual feats, but my object is only to demonstrate his kindly deportment toward myself, when I was weak and he was strong. He would not even approach his food till I had satisfied myself; would even turn out of his warm bed to give place to me, and appeared (like my master) to feel for my growing infirmities. I have noticed a large rat composedly washing his face on his back, while Nero appeared to feel proud of the confidence placed in him, while he never even dreamed of offering him any molestation. He was as good a rat-killer as myself, and equally delighted in the sport; but he never offered to touch those who had thrown themthemselves on his generosity. I have seen my master place a live rat on his nose, telling not to touch it, which order he never disobeyed; "but the instant the word "kill" was announced, he immediately destroyed him. He might even be left loose in a room with a number of rats, and if he were ordered to let them alone, they were perfectly safe, but on a given signal, instantaneous death was dealt out to the whole party. He might safely be trusted with any living thing, as he never would injure what he was ordered to guard, and the single word "Stop!" was at all times sufficient to arrest his most determined attack. In fact, he appeared to live for the benefit of others, almost regardless of his own private interests. His benignant looks spoke volumes of kindness, while his threatening glance forbade unwarranted confidence in his generosity. To *me* he was indeed a friend, his attachment increasing as my powers of reciprocation diminished. Well might he be termed my successor! I had instructed him in all his performances, had restrained him in his inconsiderate movements, and seconded him in all his praiseworthy emotions. As I grew old and helpless, he amply restored all that I had expended upon him, his cheerful attentions enlivening my incapacitated and drooping old age.

CHAPTER XLVII.

TIGER'S LAST MOMENTS, IN PRESENCE OF HIS MASTER AND HIS FRIEND "NERO."

I am now in my seventeenth year—a patriarchal age, to which few of my brethren have ever attained. The days of our years are about twelve or fourteen, and if any of us *by chance* attain the age of fifteen, the last four years of our lives are generally devoted to indolence and inactivity. But up to the age of fourteen I was capable of performing all my duties. After this period, I was of little use to my master or amusement to myself. Though to the very last I was vigilant and faithful in performing my daily routine of duties, still, as Nero was youthful, active, and intelligent, I was seldom called to any arduous undertaking, being permitted to indulge myself as I pleased, as a fitting reward for my long and valuable services. As I grew weaker and weaker, deafer and deafer, blinder and blinder, I had little left me but to ponder over past events, and retrace my history from the first cat I encountered at the dwelling of Mr. Richard Marks, down to my feline slaughters in the abode of the disappointed Schlachtenmeister—from the important epoch when I was hurried off from his lordship's stable, (shortly after my being ushered into life,) up to the sleepless hours when death was gradually winding his cords around my lingering and reasoning instinct. I occasionally started in my sleep, dreaming that the hogs were to be driven out, the rats were to be killed, the wolf was to be dislodged; upon which I would creep around in search of my foes, when my friend Nero's kindly salutation would assure me that all was right, and I would again lay me down to snooze. At other times, in my reveries, I romped with Soto, Roswell, and Truffle, hunted with Manso or Blanco, or flirted with my favorite Vick. Then I would suddenly spring up, and fancy the horrid Johnny was come to disturb my repose, or that Tripey was bidding me a last farewell. Then I was rocked in the boisterous ocean, confined in a hopeless dungeon, or having my head drawn into the domicil of an enraged snapping-turtle. I now seldom accompanied my master in his wonted travels, as he was fearful of my getting into trouble, knowing that my unabated courage was more than a match for my toothless gums.

As the last year of my life was spent in the city, I greatly missed my country rambles, and regretted the amusing ing scenes in which I had formed so conspicuous a part. But, after all, it mattered but little, as my taste for roving was well-nigh past, and my powers of endurance were vanished. Behold me now a battered veteran, the hero of a thousand fights, indented with scars, which my withering flesh renders every day more visible; a pair of once bright, blooming eyes, now lustreless and dull; ears, once quick of hearing, now reverberating with a hundred medley sounds; limbs, once elastic at the very echo of my master's voice, now stiffened and tottering; a skin, once white as snow and smooth as velvet, now become shabby, rough, and sightless. Even as I hobble along, my master is accused of cruelty in not curtailing my pitiful existence, and the finger of scorn is pointed at my trembling remains. I am no longer patted, caressed, and flattered, though all remark that I must have been a *good 'un.* In spite of all these withering indications, I was still as fond and faithful as ever, regretting only that I was unable to render any active service to my protector. I have nothing now left me but to reconsider my past life. I have served my master faithfully, have never resented his corrections nor disputed his advice; have clung to him fearlessly, in prosperity and adversity. Thus while the quivering throes of death are creeping over my wasted form, I feel

I can die in peace. But my master is going forth—I must accompany him once more before I depart. I totter on his footsteps, but my spirit faints, and I sink in my last and dying effort. He takes me in his arms, places me in my bed, bidding me lie down in peace, convincing me of his enduring friendship and esteem. The faithful Nero stands beside me in mournful silence, as my life slowly and softly ebbs away; he bids me be of good cheer, as we faintly echo our final adieu, and Tiger dies in the seventeenth year of his age, deeply lamented by all who had the pleasure of his acquaintance; and now

> "He lays like a warrior taking his rest,
> "With his canine pelt around him."

What shall we add in honor of his memory? He was truly a great and *good* dog; and may his worthy example promote the welfare of the whole canine fraternity, by convincing their benefactors that well-trained dogs will insure pleasure, comfort, profit, and safety to those who may deem them worthy of education and refinement.

THE END.

NOTICE.

Francis Butler has removed from 205 Water-street to 29 Fulton-street, in the basement, between Water and Pearl-streets, New-York, and takes the liberty of informing his friends and the public in general, that he has constantly on hand a large assortment of all the CHOICE BREEDS OF DOGS, both for sale and stock, viz:—

Mammoth Newfoundlands, St. Bernards, Broken Pointers and Setters, Hounds, King Charles and Hunting Spaniels, Scotch and English Terriers, English and Italian Greyhounds, Shepherd-Dogs, Bull-Terriers, Poodles, Watch-Dogs, etc.

All dogs will be warranted to answer the purposes for which they are recommended, and (if required) forwarded to any part of the world.

Butler's Mange Liniment and Flea Exterminator,

Is warranted a certain and speedy cure for Mange, all sores, wounds, and diseases of the skin in dogs; beautifying and restoring the hair. No dog will ever be troubled with fleas, where this is occasionally used. It immediately allays all irritation of the skin, and its influence is almost magical in the reproduction of hair. No vermin can exist in its presence, and no dog, however delicate, can be in any way injured by it.

Price 50 *cents per Bottle.*

www.ingramcontent.com/pod-product-compliance
Lightning Source LLC
LaVergne TN
LVHW021426110826
845150LV00007B/2109

* 9 7 8 1 4 2 5 5 0 7 1 3 8 *